POSTMORTEM

by Ken Ludwig

SAMUEL FRENCH, INC.
45 WEST 25TH STREET   NEW YORK 10010
7623 SUNSET BOULEVARD   HOLLYWOOD 90046
LONDON   TORONTO

PostMortem was first presented at the American Stage Festival, Milford, New Hampshire in July, 1983 with the following cast:

Macready ....Ross Patterson
Bobby Carlyle .... Richard Backus
May Dison...Kristin Griffith
Marion Barrett ....Alice White
Leo Barrett..George Ede
William Gillette..................................Patrick Horgan
Lilly Warner...................................Helen Lloyd Breed
Louise Parradine...........................Carol Mayo Jenkins
Directed by Larry Carpenter
Set design by John Falabella
Costume design by David Murin
Lighting by John Gisondi

The play was subsequently presented at the Cleveland Playhouse on January 18, 1985 with the following cast:

Macready ....Harold Merton
Bobby Carlyle ....Wayne S. Turney
May Dison... Catherine Long
Marion Barrett ....Cassandra Wolfe
Leo Barrett..John Buck, Jr.
William Gillette...........................Thomas S. Oleniacz
Lilly Warner...............................Providence Hollander
Louise Parradine................................Sharon Bicknell
Directed by Dennis Zacek
Set design and lighting by Richard Gould
Costume design by Frances Blau

Biographical Note

William Gillette was one of the best-loved American actors of the late nineteenth and early twentieth centuries. After scoring a few early successes, most notably in his own play, Secret Service, a melodrama of the American Civil War, Gillette wrote Sherlock Holmes in 1899 in collaboration with Sir Arthur Conan Doyle. The play, starring Gillette as the master detective, was an immediate hit on both sides of the Atlantic and was revived frequently by Gillette over the next thirty years. (It was also revived with great success by the Royal Shakespeare Company in 1976 starring John Wood and Philip Locke as Holmes and Moriarty.) Much of what we associate with Sherlock Holmes to this day was popularized by Gillette for his stage role, including the deerstalker cap and the meerschaum pipe.

Largely on his profits from Sherlock Holmes, Gillette—ever an eccentric—built a castle on 115 acres of land in southern Connecticut. It was patterned after a medieval Rhenish fortress, complete with crenelated battlements, took five years to build and was completed in 1919. It was here that Gillette not infrequently brought the cast of his latest New York revival for a weekend of leisure, good food and old world elegance.

Following Gillette's death in 1937, "Gillette Castle," as it came to be known, was opened to visitors by the State of Connecticut.

CHARACTERS
(In order of appearance)

Macready - a butler
Bobby Carlyle - an actor and man-about-town
May Dison - an ingenue
Marion Barrett - an actress, Gillette's sister
Leo Barrett - Marion's husband, plays Professor
  Moriarty
William Gillette - writer and star of *Sherlock
    Holmes*
Lilly Warner - Gillette's aunt
Louise Parradine - a former actress

SYNOPSIS OF SCENES

The action takes place in the living room of
"Gillette Castle," home of William Gillette, in
southern Connecticut.

ACT I

Scene 1: A Saturday night in April 1922, about
              11:30
Scene 2: An hour later
Scene 3: A half-hour later

ACT II

Scene 1: The following evening, about 6:15
Scene 2: That night, about 10 o'clock

Setting

The living room of "Gillette Castle" in Hadlyme, Connecticut, home of William Gillette.

The room is expansive and eccentric, with rough fieldstone walls and a nineteen-foot ceiling supported by massive oak beams. Upstage center are two French doors, which lead to a flagstone terrace. There are double doors, stage right, leading to a reception hall and the front door of the house. The onstage doors are of carved white oak. A staircase, stage right of the French doors, leads to a landing and then, at a right angle, to a balcony, which connects to an offstage hall. At stage left are another pair of double doors, leading to the dining room, billiard room and conservatory. Between these doors and the French doors is a sideboard surmounted by bookshelves that fold back at the touch of a button to create an elaborate bar. A chandelier hangs from the ceiling, and its lights are controlled by switches in the form of carved oak handles near all the doors.

Despite this imposing frame, the room has a certain homey charm. It contains at least one wing-back chair, an electric gramophone (cabinet style), two or three tables and lamps, and a sofa covered in chintz and piled with colorful throw pillows. Behind the sofa is a drop-leaf table;

and near the doors to the hall stands a sturdy, attractive desk with a mirror above it.

Hanging on the wall above the staircase landing is a large portrait of a beautiful woman in her mid 30's.

Finally, in various places around the room are scattered the great mementos of Sherlock Holmes, including the Persian slipper filled with shag tobacco, the deerstalker cap and the meerschaum pipe. On the desk, the Stradivarius is propped carelessly against the famous scrapbooks. And a large dagger with a jeweled handle hangs on one of the walls.

ACT I

Scene 1

SCENE: A Saturday night in April, 1922, about 11:30.

While the LIGHTS are down, we hear the sound of a CAR squealing to a halt. Two CAR DOORS slam; then a few seconds later, as the LIGHTS come up, the front DOORBELL is buzzing. The room is empty. The BELL buzzes again, several times, insistently. Finally MACREADY, the butler, enters from the dining room. Stooped and whiskered, pushing retirement, he plods through the room.

MACREADY. *(With a broad Scots accent.)* I'm on me way...I'm on me way!...Keep yer knickers on...*(He unbolts the door to the hall and exits. The DOORBELL continues to buzz, accompanied now by loud BANGING with the door knocker. We hear the sound of VOICES in the hall; and a moment later BOBBY CARLYLE bounds into the room and looks around. He's in his early 30's, good-looking with a boyish face,*

11

and wears a stylish motoring coat and cap, complete with rakish goggles.)

BOBBY. Ha ha! Victory at last, sweet victory! *(Calling off right.)* We beat him!

(MAY DISON enters, followed by MACREADY. She's a pretty, strong-minded girl in her mid 20's. Throughout the scene, she seems troubled and nervous, though she tries to hide it. She is also, at the moment, slightly dishevelled.)

BOBBY. *(To Macready.)* Gillette isn't here yet, is he?

MACREADY. Not yet, sir —

BOBBY. I knew it!

MACREADY. —but I wouldna thought he'd be vury long —

BOBBY. *(To MAY.)* An hour and forty-three minutes. What do you think of that?

MAY. You really wouldn't want to know.

BOBBY. Just wait 'til you see his face! And then, of course, he'll pretend he didn't even try to win. *(He tosses his cap and gloves carelessly on a chair.)*

MAY. You might have put up the top.

BOBBY. Well you didn't blow away, did you.

MAY. I almost fell out! You're such a lunatic with that...machine.

BOBBY. A Stutz Torpedo with dual valves, six cylinders, balloon tires and a folding

windscreen, and she calls it a "machine."...Who
are you? (*This to Macready, who is gathering
their coats.*)

MACREADY. Macready, sir. Anything yer
wantin, joost call Macready.

BOBBY. I mean where's Bates?

MACREADY. In hospital, sir.

BOBBY. Nothing serious –?

MACREADY. Naemonia, sir. They say he's
makin progress, but I wouldna trust em. He'd
have t'be a boog-eyed corpse before they'd even
look at im –

BOBBY. But he'll be all right –?

MACREADY. Aye sir. Unless he croaks.

MAY. Oh.

MACREADY. Mae own Lucy—tough as
leather, she was—she had it before they laid er
out—

BOBBY. Ah –

MACREADY. But the plain of it is, she hadna
looked better in forty years when they took her
t'hospital. And then her loongs filled with
myucous and she starts t'spittin up blood –

BOBBY. I see –

MACREADY. And the next day she's gooterin
and moanin like the livin dead –

BOBBY. Thank you, Macready. We get the
picture.

MACREADY. Oh. Aye sir. (*He starts off with
their coats, then turns and starts back.*) Now if yer

wantin any refreshments, sir, I can make ya one
of them...

BOBBY. We'll help ourselves.

MACREADY. (*Groping.*) ...cocktails.

BOBBY. Thanks.

MACREADY. Aye sir... (*He exits glumly to
the hall. BOBBY watches him leave.*)

MAY. (*Looking around.*) My God, what a
place.

BOBBY. Mm. Distinctly maniacal.
(*Troubled –*) A year later and it feels like I never
left. (*Pause.*) Hey, May—watch this. (*He pushes
a button near the bookshelves and the bar swings
open.*) A spot of gin?

MAY. All right.

(*As BOBBY pours the drinks, MAY looks around
the room, caught up in its eccentricities.*)

MAY. He got a standing ovation tonight. Did
you see it?

BOBBY. Gillette? I don't know why they
bother. After twenty years playing Sherlock
Holmes he could do it in his sleep. I mean, he's
good all right, but –

(*MAY has by now noticed a large handle set in a
panel near the French doors. She pulls it
down and the room goes BLACK.*)

BOBBY. Hey, watch it! (*The LIGHTS come back on.*)

BOBBY. Having fun?

MAY. Sorry.

BOBBY. (*Still making the drinks.*) Anyway, if you ask me, the old boy's getting obsessed. Do you know, he's started wearing that deerstalker hat outside, on the street. With the cape from Act One. The whole works. I mean, the man actually believes that he's Sherlock Holmes.

MAY. He does not.

BOBBY. His fiancee—before she died, he used to call her "Watson." In front of everybody.

MAY. Oh stop it.

(*MACREADY enters.*)

BOBBY. He did! I'm telling you, the man is crackers. Not just eccentric. I'm talking bats in the belfry. Gonzo...(*By this time MAY, but not BOBBY, has seen MACREADY standing in the doorway.*)

MAY. Bobby –

BOBBY. They'll carry him off soon, wearing a dress, screaming "It's me! Sherlock Holmes! But I'm in disguise!" –

MAY. Bobby!

BOBBY. Hm? (*He turns and sees MACREADY.*) Oh.

MAY. He was only joking...

BOBBY. Well, now...of course I was...And I'm sure that our old pal, Mr. Macready, wouldn't repeat a little idle chatter among friends. (*He presses a five dollar bill into MACREADY's hand.*) Hm?

MACREADY. Nos'r.

BOBBY. Of course not.

MACREADY. If I cud joost have the key t'yer boot, sir.

BOBBY. Oh. Of course. Very kind...(*He hands him the key.*) You'll watch the golf clubs, will you? New set.

MACREADY. Aye sir...(*He stands his ground, looking mournfully at the five dollars.*) I'll take the bags, ya see, oopstairs, t'yer rooms...

BOBBY. (*Giving him another bill.*) Yes, please do.

MACREADY. (*Happy now.*) Best to you, sir. Miss. (*He exits to the hall, closing the door behind him.*)

MAY. No wonder you're always short.

BOBBY. The old thief. He's probably at the keyhole now. Cigarette?

MAY. Thanks. (*He offers her a cigarette, takes one himself—his last—then crumples the pack and leaves it on the table.*)

BOBBY. I hope they get here soon. I'm starving.

MAY. You're always starving.

BOBBY. (*Sexy, trying to kiss her.*) Yes, I know. Hungry for love...

MAY. Bobby. Not here. I told you.

BOBBY. ...Sorry. (*Pause.*) Hey. Guess what?

MAY. (*Uninterested; lighting her cigarette.*) What.

BOBBY. I brought the camera. Thought you might take me with the great Sarah, tomorrow night. Bobby Carlyle meets Sarah Bernhardt. Historic event. Crowds cheer, Sarah swoons. Autographs upon request...

MAY. Is that Maude? (*She's standing near the stairs, looking up at the portrait.*)

BOBBY. Hm?

MAY. Maude Redding. Is that her?

BOBBY. (*Seeing the portrait for the first time.*) ...So it is.

MAY. She's beautiful.

BOBBY. Was beautiful. She killed herself.

MAY. Yes, I know.

BOBBY. Worst damn night of my entire life. Of course, I suppose it wasn't so hot for her, either.

MAY. What happened? I mean, you were here.

BOBBY. Oh I was here all right. But, like everybody else, I was sleeping. It was three in the morning.

MAY. Was it...in her bedroom?

BOBBY. No, it was down here. Out on the terrace.

MAY. You heard the shot –?

BOBBY. Mm. Sort of. I mean, it woke me up, and then I ran down here, with Leo and Marion, and ...well, Gillette was kneeling beside the body and...there she was. Just lying there.

MAY. She must have looked awful.

BOBBY. No, she didn't. She looked beautiful. Except for one perfect little hole in her forehead. (*Pause.*) I don't suppose we could change the subject.

MAY. Sure.

(*BOBBY, obviously a bit rattled, goes to the bar and pours himself a drink. Pause.*)

MAY. You were in love with her, weren't you?

BOBBY. ...Says who?

MAY. Nobody special. It's just a rumor, I guess. (*Pause.*) Is it true?

BOBBY. And if it is...will you be madly jealous?

MAY. (*Coldly.*) No.

BOBBY. Well in that case, I'm not telling.

MAY. Who cares. I just wondered.

BOBBY. You really do look like her, you know. A lot. So maybe the truth is, I don't care about you at all. I'm just reliving the past— necking with you and dreaming of Maude...

MAY. (*Cold as ice.*) Is that supposed to be funny? Because it's not. It's ugly.

BOBBY. You really are a pill today. I hope you know that.

MAY. Well it's too bad, isn't it?

BOBBY. Yes it is. Now I'll have to jolly you up. (*He heads for the gramophone. During the following, he flips through the records, reading the titles, chooses one and puts it on the platter.*)

MAY. Oh, please —

BOBBY. (*Jaunty.*) So, what'll it be? Rudy Vallee singing "Oh, Oh, Daddy"?

MAY. Bobby —

BOBBY. Or Paul Whiteman and his orchestra: "I Left Her on The Beach in Honolulu"-

MAY. I'm not dancing —

BOBBY. Trixie Smith and the Jazz Hounds, "I've Saved All My Lovin' for You." That sounds promising...

MAY. (*Her anger and anxiety mounting.*) Bobby, stop it...

BOBBY. Aha! Hold onto your hats, music lovers. It's Mabel Kelly and Her Bachelor Girls playing that all-time classic, (*Positioning the tone arm -*) the one, the only...the Charleston!

(*The opening bars of the CHARLESTON blare from the gramophone.*)

BOBBY. (*Dancing over to her.*) All right, let's go! Three days straight, we'll set a record! Ha ha! (*He grabs her and starts to dance.*)

MAY. (*Resisting.*) Bobby, not here! ...

BOBBY. Oh come on...

MAY. Please —

BOBBY. Then how about a kiss –?
MAY. No!...
BOBBY. (*Pressing her.*) Just one...

(*Suddenly, she pushes him away violently and screams at him, vehemently, half hysterical.*)

MAY. ...I said STOP it!!

(*Stunned, he stops dead. MAY is panting with anger. They stare at each other. Without a word, he walks to the gramophone and turns it off.*)

BOBBY. (*Quietly.*) Right. (*Pause. He strolls away toward the French doors. She sighs deeply, taking hold of herself. Finally –*)
MAY. (*Quietly.*) Bobby...I'm sorry.

(*At this moment, a CAR is heard pulling up outside.*)

BOBBY. Well...it's about time they got here. (*He looks out the window.*)
MAY. It's this place or something. I—I don't know. (*No reply.*) Hey. Forgive me?
BOBBY. I'll think about it.
MAY. Thanks a lot. (*MAY goes to the mirror to fix her hair. Meanwhile, BOBBY realizes that he has no cigarettes and looks for MAY's purse.*)

BOBBY. It's too bad, actually. Just imagine—
—we could have been lying on the sofa, necking,
when Gillette walked in. That would have curled
his hair.

MAY. (*Unhappily.*) He couldn't care less.

BOBBY. That's what you think. Do you have
any cigarettes? (*He picks up her purse.*)

MAY. Yes...No! No I don't. (*Running to
him.*) Give me that—!

(*BOBBY has by now opened the purse and seen
what's inside. MAY sees that he has and stops
dead. Gingerly, he pulls a revolver from her
purse and holds it up between two fingers.
Pause.*)

BOBBY. ...Jesus Christ.

MAY. Put it back.

BOBBY. May...? (*He eyes her, curiously.*)

MAY. Here, give it to me. (*She takes the gun
from him, then her purse, puts the gun inside and
snaps the purse shut.*) I—I wanted protection.

BOBBY. From me?

MAY. No, stupid. In New York. The city...

BOBBY. Oh.

MAY. Just forget it.

BOBBY. If you say so.

(*He turns away as MAY, still shaken, retreats to
the other side of the room to pull herself
together. A moment later the door to the hall*

opens and LEO and MARION BARRETT enter. MARION—GILLETTE's sister— plays Madge Larrabee in Sherlock Holmes. *She's about 45, has good features and a brassy, likeable way about her. LEO, her husband, plays Professor Moriarty. A few years older than MARION, he's the perfect match for her.)*

MARION. Greetings, all! Time for fun!

BOBBY. (*Resuming his usual manner.*) Well what do you know. At long last...

LEO. Listen to him, the new speed king. (*During the following, MARION and LEO remove their coats.*)

BOBBY. Did you have to push it?

MARION. Another minute and we'd have been soaked. He drives like an old woman.

LEO. (*To MAY.*) Hello dear. You were wonderful tonight. Just wonderful.

MAY. Thanks. You too.

LEO. Oh, my usual round of boos and hisses. That's what I like about playing villains. If the audience really hates you, it means they love you. And if they love you, they hate you.

MARION. After all these years, darling, they would boo you as Peter Pan.

MAY. I wouldn't.

BOBBY. I would.

LEO. (*To MAY.*) Did you survive in that contraption of his?

MAY. I kept my eyes closed.

LEO. (*Laughing.*) I'd have jumped.

BOBBY. (*To MARION.*) Just wait 'til he gets one.

MARION. I'll divorce him and the car both. In one action. Now don't dawdle, get me a drink.

LEO. Two.

MAY. Three.

MARION. (*Collapsing on the chaise.*) All weekend, just think of it! No audience and no cues!

BOBBY. (*At the bar.*) And no makeup.

MARION. Oh God forbid. I'd rather shoot myself.

(*Pause. BOBBY, MAY and LEO look at MARION in silence.*)

MARION. ...Oops.

LEO. You certainly have a way with words, my dear.

MARION. Sorry. I forgot. Hallowed ground...

LEO. Damn stupid, if you ask me.

MARION. (*Flaring up.*) I said I was sorry!

LEO. Not you. Him! Your brother.

MARION. (*Mollified.*) Oh.

LEO. A year to the day since...Maude shot herself, and he has a party.

BOBBY. Is it? My God...

MAY. Maybe he doesn't realize.

MARION. Oh he knows, believe me. Willie doesn't miss a thing.

LEO. Very poor taste, if you ask me. I told him so, too.

BOBBY. What did he say?

LEO. He said "Life, old boy, is for the living, not the dead."

MARION. Well good for him. At least he's being sensible for a change.

LEO. Sensible? I'm glad you think so. They were engaged to be married, for God's sake.

MARION. Well he can't go on mourning her forever.

LEO. Suppose that one year ago today, I had shot myself through the head. Would you be having a party, dear?

MARION. Well no, I wouldn't. I mean, my God, who would I get to make the dip?

LEO. (*Not unamused.*) Yes...Well, taste aside, I must admit I simply cannot wait for tomorrow night. Though how the hell the Ashtons got Sarah Bernhardt to go to their party, I will never know.

BOBBY. Well, according to *Variety* –

MARION. Here it comes.

LEO. He has it memorized.

BOBBY. According to *Variety*...Ashton Senior has some money in the tour. And she's staying at his place all weekend.

LEO. She's there now? It's just down the road.

BOBBY. That's what it said.

LEO. Oh, my God. I think I'll cry.

MARION. Not here, darling. Wait and do it at Sarah's feet. She'll be so pleased.

LEO. You needn't be jealous, dear. She's even older than you are.

BOBBY. Is she really so wonderful? I mean, everyone hears about Sarah Bernhardt—

LEO. Bite your tongue. I saw her in *Camille* almost thirty years ago and realized instantly that I'd seen a legend. It's the voice. No one can touch her.

MARION. Thank you, dear.

(*MACREADY enters unnoticed to collect the coats.*)

MAY. Mr. Gillette has a picture of her, in his dressing room. Signed to him.

MARION. I think he played with her once.

LEO. Did he? The lucky dog.

MARION. In Shakespeare, darling.

BOBBY. Where is he, anyway? Ashamed to face me?

LEO. I shouldn't think so.

MARION. Isn't he here?

BOBBY. You came with him.

MARION. No we didn't. I thought he came with you.

BOBBY. No. (*Beat.*)

MARION. Don't tell me we left him at the theatre! (*She can't help laughing at this.*)

BOBBY. Macready, has Mr. Gillette arrived?

MACREADY. I havna seen him, sir—

MAY. Oh no!

MARION. Where's Bates?

BOBBY. He's sick.

MACREADY. Naemonia, madam. He's in hospital—

BOBBY. He had his car at the theatre, I know that—

MAY. It might have broken down...

BOBBY. Now that would be funny!

MAY. I don't see what's funny about it! He could have had an accident.

LEO. (*Authoritatively.*) He did not have an accident. (*They all look at him.*)

MARION. How do you know?

LEO. In fact, ladies and gentlemen, he arrived here safely, and our friend, Mr. Macready, saw him do so.

MACREADY. I didna see him, sir, I swear it—

LEO. You did, though, didn't you? (*Threateningly, he approaches MACREADY, who backs away.*) You saw him enter this house, you knew that Bates was not in the hospital— (*Suddenly, LEO grabs the dagger from the wall and turns on MACREADY.*)

MARION. Leo!

MAY. (*Simultaneously.*) No!

(*MACREADY, frightened and desperate, pulls a gun from his coat. His hand is shaking.*)

MACREADY. Get back! Get back! I'll shoot ya daed, I swear ta God! (*He fires the gun into the ceiling as a warning. The others scream and then freeze.*)

LEO. (*Calmly.*) The game is up, Macready. Shall I call the police? (*Beat.*)

MACREADY. Leo, you bastard, I could have had them going all night! (*He straightens up and pulls off his wig.*)

MARION. Willie!

MAY. Mr. Gillette!

BOBBY. Oh, God...

GILLETTE. (*To LEO, in his Sherlock Holmes voice.*) I should have known you'd spot it, Professor Moriarty.

LEO. (*His Moriarty voice.*) After twenty years, Mr. Holmes, I could recognize you under a haystack.

MARION. (*Shaken, angry.*) Willie, for Christ's sake! Can't you just walk in the door like other people!

GILLETTE. But, Marion dear, this is much more fun. (*During the following, he removes his whiskers and peels the spirit gum from his face. He uses a towel from the bar to remove his makeup, then removes his Macready coat and dons the suit coat that has been draped over the desk chair since the scene began.*)

MARION. Jesus Christ...

LEO. Calm yourself, dear.

GILLETTE. Now what did you think, honestly? Don't be kind.

MAY. It was wonderful! I was fooled completely. I never would have guessed.

GILLETTE. "If music be the food of love, play on." (*He kisses her hand.*)

LEO. "That instant was I turned into a hart, And my desires, like fell and cruel hounds, E'er since pursue me."

BOBBY. I had my suspicions.

MAY. Oh, you did not.

GILLETTE. "The heart is deceitful above all else, and desperately wicked."

LEO. *Othello?*

GILLETTE. Jeremiah. The Good Book.

LEO. Showoff.

MARION. (*To LEO.*) You really should have let him be. We could have ordered him around all night.

LEO. Now that would have been fun.

BOBBY. (*Quietly, to GILLETTE.*) I believe you have ten dollars of mine.

GILLETTE. (*Scots, confidentially.*) I havna seen it, sir. Ya moosta dropped it.

MARION. Where is Bates, anyway?

GILLETTE. He's on vacation. Living it up in Atlantic City. I think I must pay him too much...

LEO. I can assure you, Gillette, speaking as an employee, you don't pay anyone too much.

(*By this time, LILLY WARNER—GILLETTE
and MARION's aunt—has appeared on the
balcony. She's in her late 60's, early 70's,
wearing a hostess gown. She speaks and
moves with the grand air of a bygone era.*)

LILLY. Well...may I enter now, Willie?
GILLETTE. Yes, dear. I'm all through.

(*She descends the staircase.*)

BOBBY. Lilly!
LEO. Well well well...
LILLY. Hello, my darlings.
MARION. Aunt Lilly, don't tell me you were
in on this.
LILLY. Not by choice, dear, I assure you. He
said, if I was down here with you, that I'd give it
away. He called me "old poker face."
MARION. Willie.
GILLETTE. Oh you know Aunt Lilly, she'd
have taken one look at me and started giggling.
She even does it on my opening nights. I can hear
it, onstage.
LILLY. Oh you cannot. (*To MAY–*) Even as a
child he liked to play dress up. When he was six
years old, he put on one of my best hats and started
prancing around, telling everyone that he was
Ellen Terry. His mother said he was a born actor.
I thought he was a transvestite.

GILLETTE. Thank you, dear. We get the point.

LILLY. Now you all must be simply starving. Shall we go inside?...

GILLETTE. Ah ah ah. Wait a moment. We certainly can't start without all the guests.

LILLY. Everyone's here, I think.

GILLETTE. No, everyone is not here, I'm afraid. And we don't want to be rude.

MARION. He's up to something.

LILLY. Sometimes I'd just like to shake him until he rattles!

LEO. I know the feeling.

GILLETTE. My dear, I have simply invited one additional guest. Most of you know her, actually. And I can assure you that the weekend simply would not be complete without her. (Pause.)

MARION. ...Louise.

GILLETTE. Very good, Marion. Excellent.

LEO. Louise.

BOBBY. (Sarcasm.) Oh great.

LILLY. Willie...

MAY. Who's Louise?

GILLETTE. Louise Parradine. (Pronounced para-dean.) She and Maude were best friends. They shared an apartment together in the city. Louise was staying here, along with the rest of us, the night that ...Maude died.

MAY. I see.

BOBBY. No, you don't. You should have been here...

GILLETTE. Louise didn't take it very well, I'm afraid. The shock. She couldn't quite...cope with it, emotionally.

BOBBY. That's an understatement. (*To MAY–*) She got hysterical. She went nuts. They had to inject her.

LEO. She had a nervous breakdown. It is not uncommon.

LILLY. Willie, dear, do you think it was wise, having her back here like this...

GILLETTE. Oh, absolutely. She's perfectly fine now.

MARION. Is she? I wonder.

GILLETTE. Oh, yes, I assure you. We had lunch together last week. I mean, she's still a bit edgy, of course.

BOBBY. I'll bet.

GILLETTE. (*Annoyed.*) I said...that she's fine.

BOBBY. ...Sure. If you say so.

LEO. People do recover from these things. All the time.

GILLETTE. Thank you, Leo. She ought to be here by now.

MAY. (*At the window.*) There's a car coming up the drive.

GILLETTE. Excellent.

MARION. If you ask me, I think it was stupid.

LEO. Marion...

MARION. (*To Gillette.*) And if she makes a scene, it's your own fault. That's all I have to say. (*A tense pause.*)

GILLETTE. (*Quietly.*) Well now you've said it, Marion. However, let me remind you that as a guest in my house, she will be treated with all due kindness and consideration. For Maude's sake, if nothing else.

LILLY. Well of course she will be. Don't argue with your sister, Willie...

GILLETTE. Excuse me. (*He exits to the hall. Pause.*)

BOBBY. I just knew this would be a fun weekend.

LEO. Oh, don't be a fool.

MAY. Is Louise in the theatre?

LEO. She was, yes. She played the maid in the current production. But of course she left the show. After that night.

BOBBY. It was that or shove her onstage in a straitjacket. (*Beat. They all look at him.*) Just joking...

(*GILLETTE appears at the hall door, carrying a suitcase, and everyone turns to him. He pauses for dramatic effect.*)

GILLETTE. (*To the unseen guest.*) Come in, my dear. Join the party.

(*A pause. Then LOUISE PARRADINE appears in the doorway. She's in her mid to late 30's, tall and strikingly beautiful, dressed extravagantly, with great elegance. She looks as though she might be the queen of one of the smaller Balkan states, the sort of female that Sherlock Holmes has encountered on more than one occasion. Her manner is refined, slightly distant and perfectly normal—with an undertone of fragile nerves.*)

LOUISE. (*Quietly.*) I'm sorry I'm late. (*Silence.*)

LILLY. Louise?...

GILLETTE. (*Delighted at the effect he's created.*) Come in, come in!

LILLY. Hello, my dear, it's lovely to see you.

LOUISE. Hello, Lilly.

LEO. Louise...welcome! (*They embrace.*)

LOUISE. (*With affection.*) Leo, you look wonderful.

LEO. Well, so do you. Just fabulous...

LOUISE. Bobby—

BOBBY. Hi. How are you?

LOUISE. I'm fine, thank you. Just fine.

GILLETTE. Louise, my dear, welcome to the Castle. (*He kisses her hand and holds it perhaps longer than necessary.*)

LOUISE. Thank you, William. (*Looking around—*) It hasn't changed a bit, has it...

MARION. Same old place, same old people.

LOUISE. (*Cool but gracious.*) Hello, Marion.

LILLY. You didn't get very wet—?

LOUISE. (*Removing her gloves.*) Not at all.

GILLETTE. It's a pity that your taxi had a flat tire.

LOUISE. That was a nuisance, just—(*She stops and thinks.*) How did you know that?

GILLETTE. I perceive it, my dear. I deduce it. How do I know that you left your apartment this evening in a terrible hurry? That you rode first class on the train from New York. (*Pause.*) How do I know that the driver of your unfortunate taxicab...was Irish?

LEO. It's gone to his brain, Lilly. Call the doctor.

MARION. Willie, for God's sake—

BOBBY. Is he right?

LOUISE. Yes.

GILLETTE. (*Modestly.*) Elementary.

MARION. Okay, Sherlock. Let's hear it.

GILLETTE. Well, it's fairly simple. The edge of a ruffled slip sticking out of her suitcase tells us plainly that she left in a rush. But of course, she always was running late—even for her entrance— so that's no surprise. And the stub that fell to the floor when she took off her gloves (*He picks it up.*) couldn't tell us more if they'd stamped Louise instead of the ticket.

BOBBY. Get to the flat tire.

GILLETTE. Well look at the woman! A meticulous dresser. An absolute vision of perfection.

LOUISE. Thank you.

GILLETTE. Surely she didn't leave her room with yellow mud caked on her left shoe. (*They all look at her shoe.*) If it was engine trouble, she would have stayed in the car. But you couldn't expect the poor fellow to jack it up while she sat inside.

MARION. I hate to ask, but what about the Irish driver?

GILLETTE. (*resigned.*) I am at pains to relate that I know all three of the East Haddam taxi drivers, and they are all Irish.

BOBBY. Fraud!

LEO. Let's burn him as a witch.

LOUISE. (*Turning to MAY, who has been staring at her critically for some time.*) How do you do?

MAY. Hello.

GILLETTE. Oh, how stupid of me. Louise Parradine, this is May Dison.

MAY. How do you do.

GILLETTE. May is our newest Alice. Fresh from a season of Shakespeare—in Cleveland, God help her.

LOUISE. (*Fascinated.*) She really does look like Maude, doesn't she? He said you did, but I thought he must be exaggerating.

MAY. I guess I must. Everyone says so.

GILLETTE. (*To MAY.*) Louise was with us in the company for over two years. She played Terese, ze French maid.

LOUISE. (*As Terese.*) "Ze cellaire of zat house! Eet ees a dreadful place. He deed not come back. He went down—he deed not come up."

GILLETTE. (*As Holmes.*) "Has he been down there long?"

LOUISE. "No—for I soon suspect—ze dreadful noise was heard. Oh—(*Covers face.*)— ze dreadful noise!"

GILLETTE. "What noise?"

LOUISE. "Ze noise!"

GILLETTE. (*Taking her by the shoulders.*) "Madam, try to be calm and answer me! What did it sound like?"

LOUISE. (*Dramatically.*) "Ze dreadful cry of a man who eez stuck down by some deadly seeng!"[*]

(*They all laugh—except MARION.*)

LILLY. Bravo!
BOBBY. Bravo!
LEO. (*Overlapping.*) Hear hear.
GILLETTE. You still remember. I'm very touched.

---

[*] From Act II, Scene 2 of *Sherlock Holmes* By William Gillette and Sir Arthur Conan Doyle.

LOUISE. That immortal prose. It will never leave me.

LEO. Have you gotten back to it yet? Acting.

(*LOUISE looks at GILLETTE, surprised that he hasn't told them.*)

LOUISE. No. No, I've changed professions, actually.

LEO. Ah. (*Pause.*)

BOBBY. Well what are you doing? It's not illegal, is it? Housebreaking...?

LOUISE. No. (*Pause.*) I've become a medium. (*Silence.*)

LILLY. Oh. How nice.

LEO. A medium—?

LOUISE. Yes.

BOBBY. You mean you...talk to dead people.

LOUISE. Things like that?

LILLY. (*To GILLETTE.*) Did you hear that, dear?

GILLETTE. Oh yes. I know all about it. She's very blessed. I've tried to reach the other side myself, actually, but alas, I haven't the gift. Not many do.

MARION. You just decided one day, that you'd become a medium—?

LOUISE. No. It isn't like that. It simply happens. The realization...

GILLETTE. Go on. Tell them.

LOUISE. (*Quietly.*) Well there isn't much to tell, really. It was in the hospital, after my breakdown, and I couldn't sleep...for several days. They gave me some pills, but it didn't help, and on the fourth night, I was lying there, alone, I suppose I was frightened, and I started to cry. I couldn't stop. I was crying so hard that I could scarcely breathe. And then I heard a voice, and I looked up, and there was Maude. She was standing by my bedside, looking down, and she took my hand. She held it...and she put me to sleep. (*Pause.*) Of course I realized, after that, that I had the gift.

(*Pause.*)

GILLETTE. (*Moved.*) How I envy you.
LEO. Yes...
GILLETTE. But of course she left out the best part.
LOUISE. I did?
GILLETTE. Tonight.
LOUISE. Oh.
MARION. (*Acidly.*) Tonight...what?
GILLETTE. Well that should be obvious, Marion. We're going to have a seance.
MAY. A seance—?
GILLETTE. Louise has very kindly consented to help us make contact with the other side. I, for one, am very excited.
MARION. Yes, I'm sure.

LOUISE. We really don't have to. If you'd rather not.

GILLETTE. Oh nonsense. They'll love it.

BOBBY. Sure. Why not? It sounds great.

GILLETTE. Now that's what I like. A man of adventure. Leo? Marion? Any objections?

(*LEO and MARION glance at each other.*)

MARION. ...Fine.

LEO. It's all right with me.

GILLETTE. Lilly?

LILLY. If you say so, dear.

GILLETTE. And that leaves...May.

(*Everyone looks at her. Pause.*)

MAY. ...Of course. Why not?

GILLETTE. Excellent. Bravo! "O brave new world that has such people in't!" Now Lilly, dear, for heaven's sake, can we have some dinner? I'm starving to death.

LILLY. Yes, of course, you all must be ravenous.

BOBBY. Now you're talking.

LEO. I think I could manage a little something...

LILLY. This way. (*She exits into the dining room.*)

LEO. (*To MARION, offering his arm.*) My dear.

MARION. Enchantée. (*She shoots GILLETTE a look as she and LEO follow LILLY.*)

(*GILLETTE and LOUISE pause for a moment and look at each other.*)

GILLETTE. Louise, my dear, thank you for coming. It's simply wonderful having you here.

LOUISE. (*Quietly.*) Thank you, William. There's nowhere else in the world I'd rather be. Believe me.

(*As they're about to exit, LOUISE pauses for a moment and looks at MAY; then she continues with GILLETTE into the dining room. MAY, troubled, has been watching them, as has BOBBY, who's standing near the bar.*)

BOBBY. What did I tell you? She's nuts. (*He turns to the bar and pours himself a last quick one. Confidentially –*) The rumor was—and you know how I hate gossip—but the rumor was that Leo had this thing for Louise, which of course teed Marion off, and Louise had some lover tucked away, but no one really knew who it was. I mean, backstage, it was like we had this Italian opera going on...

(*But MAY hasn't heard a word he's said. She stares into the dining room. Mechanically,*

*she picks up her purse and is about to leave,
when she feels her gun through the cloth. She
hesitates for a moment, then walks into the
dining room.)*

BOBBY. (*Oblivious to her exit.*)...But of
course it all took care of itself in the end. Maude
was dead, and Louise went round the bend, and
...May?...(*He turns around and realizes that
she's gone.*) Thanks a lot. (*He sighs and drains
his drink.*) A fellow could drop dead around here,
and nobody would even notice. (*He smiles at his
joke, straightens his tie and walks into the dining
room, closing the door behind him.*)

(*The LIGHTS fade.*)

End of Scene

Scene 2

An hour later.
*A bright flash of LIGHTNING, a crack of
    THUNDER, then the LIGHTS come up.*
*The women are having their coffee. LILLY and
    MAY are sitting on the sofa, MARION is idly
    sorting through the records next to the
    gramophone, and LOUISE stands gazing out
    of the windows, preoccupied. Outside, it's*

RAINING heavily, beating against the windows. From time to time throughout the scene we hear the WIND howling and the rumble of THUNDER.

LILLY. (*After a pause.*) And I suppose they have to be dead, don't they?

LOUISE. Hm? Yes. But we prefer to say "passed over." The spirit never dies. It lives forever.

MARION. Well that's reassuring.

LILLY. (*To LOUISE.*) Do you feel in the mood, dear? Can you tell yet?

LOUISE. I'm afraid that mood has nothing to do with it.

MAY. Do you have a control?

LILLY. A control?

MARION. A contact. A sort of spiritual go-between.

LOUISE. (*To MAY.*) Yes. I do. Her name is Katie. Katie King. She was a medium herself, in London. Quite well known, in fact. She was murdered by her lover in 1880.

LILLY. How very unpleasant.

MAY. Do you ever get frightened? When it— happens?

LOUISE. Sometimes. (*She lights a cigarette, not too steadily.*) When...Maude first came to me that night, I thought...well, I thought I'd gone insane. Truly insane. That was frightening.

(*Pause.*) But then sometimes nothing happens at all. We might just sit here, in the dark.

MAY. Nothing?

LOUISE. If no one wants to get through. I'm afraid it's really out of my hands.

(*From the dining room we hear a burst of LAUGHTER.*)

MARION. I'd like to know what they're up to.

LILLY. Just being men, my dear. Which is quite enough.

MARION. I wonder what they'd say if they came out and found us all sozzled, smoking cigars.

LILLY. (*To LOUISE.*) Have you seen the show yet, dear? Since you left us?

LOUISE. No, I haven't. I'm going next week.

LILLY. You'd better, or Willie won't speak to you.

LOUISE. You'd think he'd be tired of playing Holmes after all these years. Bored to death.

LILLY. Bored? My dear, he absolutely revels in it. Of course, he does play other parts between revivals.

MAY. He's wonderful in it. He really is.

MARION. And this from a girl who kisses him passionately every night.

MAY. On cue!

MARION. No wonder Bobby's jealous.

MAY. Marion —

LILLY. Now don't tease.

LOUISE. I can still see Maude doing it. Do you remember? Turning slowly front, then around to face him, meeting his eyes...

MARION. Well this kid's even better. Believe me.

MAY. I wish I'd seen her. She must have been something.

LOUISE. She was. The best.

MAY. They said you shared an apartment with her.

LOUISE. For almost five years. We had two little rooms together, and we spent the entire first year decorating them. Two rooms.

LILLY. (*Sadly.*) Such a tragedy... (*Pause.*)

LOUISE. She would have loved being here this weekend. She adored Bernhardt. We both did. We saw her together the year we met. At Booth's Theatre, in Rostand's *The Eagle.* The Great Sarah was sixty-five, playing a teenage boy, and we sat there in the balcony and cried our eyes out like two silly schoolgirls.

LILLY. She certainly played a lot of men, didn't she? I saw her do Hamlet once, years ago.

LOUISE. *Le travesti.* That's what the French call it. Women playing men. It's an old tradition.

LILLY. Well I'm sure it isn't healthy at all.

LOUISE. There's a story that when Sarah was playing Hamlet in Paris. a young girl saw her and fell madly in love with her. Sent her flowers and poems every day. The girl's parents were upset and asked Sarah to do something. So she sent for the girl and met her in her dressing room in an old bathrobe, without any makeup on, looking tired and haggard. "Take a look," she said. "This is your handsome prince."

MAY. What happened?

LOUISE. The girl drowned herself.

(Pause. The dining room door opens and the men appear, led by GILLETTE, who's in exuberant spirits.)

GILLETTE. Ladies...

MARION. Well it's about time!

GILLETTE. It is indeed. (*In high Victorian style* –) "'Tis now the very witching time of night, When churchyards yawn and hell itself breathes out Contagion to this world... –"

LILLY. Yes, dear –

GILLETTE. – "Now could I drink hot blood, And do such bitter business as the day Would quake to look on." Ha! Oh, I really should have done a Hamlet. Leo, what do you say? We'll play it together next season. You'll do Polonius.

LEO. (*At the bar, pouring himself a drink.*) Oh sure. You get all the curtain calls, and I get stabbed up the arras...

MARION. Leo...

GILLETTE. Ooh, that's rather good, actually. I'll have to steal that one.

BOBBY. (*Smoking a cigar.*) I just know this is going to be great fun!

MAY. Bobby...

BOBBY. (*To Louise.*) I don't mean fun, exactly...

LOUISE. I understand.

GILLETTE. (*To himself.*) We'll need a table...

LILLY. I thought the dropleaf—

GILLETTE. Yes, that'll do. Louise?...

LOUISE. Yes, that's fine.

GILLETTE. Gentlemen.

BOBBY. Righto.

(*During the next few minutes, the men carry the dropleaf table to the center of the room, open it and place seven chairs around it, carrying some of them in from the dining room. The dialogue continues without interruption.*)

LEO. Lilly. It really was a superb dinner.

BOBBY. Hear hear! Better than ever.

LILLY. Thank you, dear. It's our new cook, Francine. She's French and quite wonderful, as long as she doesn't cook brains and things. You know the French—adventurous, I'm sure, but so disgusting.

BOBBY. I quite like brains, actually.

LEO. (*Stops what he's doing and looks at BOBBY.*) Next time ask for a second helping.

MAY. (*To GILLETTE.*) Can I help?

GILLETTE. Absolutely. Grab a chair.

BOBBY. I wish I knew someone who'd died recently. All of my friends are so healthy.

LEO. How sad for you.

LILLY. Our postman died last month. But I don't think he'd want to see us.

BOBBY. It's possible.

LILLY. No, I don't think so. Willie forgot to tip him last Christmas.

MARION. Then maybe he will come back, with his hand out, special delivery.

(*A flash of LIGHTNING and a crash of THUNDER. The storm is on top of them now.*)

GILLETTE. (*Surveying the table and chairs.*) Well that should do it...

LEO. Looks all right.

GILLETTE. Louise?

(*LOUISE is standing alone at the foot of the stairs, gazing up at the portrait of MAUDE. The others look at her.*)

LOUISE. ...She was much more beautiful than that. It doesn't do her justice.

LILLY. (*Sadly.*) It was painted after her death, from photographs. It's never as good that way.

LOUISE. No. It isn't. (*She turns.*) Are we ready?

GILLETTE. I think so.

BOBBY. All set.

GILLETTE. We place ourselves in your able hands.

LOUISE. (*Quietly.*) Thank you. Will you all sit at the table, please?

GILLETTE. Any particular order?

LOUISE. No.

(*They all take their seats, except LOUISE. Her chair is at the back of the table, so that when she sits, she'll be facing the audience. The seating, from her left, is GILLETTE, LILLY, BOBBY, MAY, MARION and LEO, who is on LOUISE's right.*)

BOBBY. (*Taking his seat, to MAY.*) I'm beginning to feel creepy already.

MAY. Bobby...

LOUISE. (*To GILLETTE, who's seated.*) The lights?

GILLETTE. Next to the door. The handle.

MARION. (*Sitting, hating every second of it.*) Now isn't this fun...

(*LOUISE moves to the French doors. By this time, everyone is seated.*)

GILLETTE. (*To Louise.*) All set.

(After a pause, LOUISE pulls the handle that serves as a LIGHT SWITCH, which turns off all the lights with the exception of a single lamp. In the semi-darkness, the LAMP throws long, weird shadows along the walls and ceiling, leaving everyone visible, though more in outline than by features. LOUISE walks to the table and pauses. She raises her right hand above the table, then lowers it slowly until her palm touches the tabletop.)

LOUISE. Please put your hands on the table, palms down. Now spread your fingers so that they're touching those of the person next to you. *(She looks at their hands to see that it's been done properly.)* That's fine. *(She pauses again, then walks slowly back to the French doors. The silence is becoming awkward...)*

BOBBY. *(Transylvanian, to MAY.)* There are two rred mardks on your neck, my dear...
MAY. Oh, please...
LILLY. *(Simultaneously.)* He's such a delinquent!
BOBBY. Sorry —
LOUISE. I must ask you to be quiet, please.
LEO. Good luck with Marion.
GILLETTE. Leo...
MARION. Does anyone know a good lawyer? And he can have the house.

(*LOUISE stands in front of the French doors,
   facing the terrace. She closes the drapes, then
   lifts her arms and places one hand at each
   side of the doors, well above her shoulders.
   She tilts her head back and begins to breathe,
   deeply, through her mouth. After a few
   seconds of this, there is a flash of white
   LIGHTNING and a clap of THUNDER,
   sharply silhouetting her body against the
   windows. She doesn't flinch. She turns,
   finally, and walks to the table, taking her
   seat between GILLETTE and LEO. She
   places her palms down on the table,
   completing the circle.*)

LOUISE. Please clear your minds and think
of nothing. You can close your eyes if it helps you.

(*LOUISE closes her eyes and breathes evenly.
   The others do likewise. All is silence. After a
   long pause, the clock CHIMES one o'clock.
   Everyone, except LOUISE, starts slightly.*)

MAY. Oh!
LILLY. Oh!
MARION. My God...

(*When they see that LOUISE is still breathing
   calmly, with her eyes closed, they resume.
   After another few seconds have passed,*

LOUISE's breathing begins to grow restless. Little by little, it increases in speed, faster and faster, until she begins gasping, almost gulping at the air. Then, quietly at first, she begins to moan. Her moaning becomes troubled, as though she's in some physical pain.)

LOUISE. No...no...no...(*Her moaning dies away. She has achieved a troubled peace. Long pause. Then, suddenly, she calls out, a scream...)*

LOUISE. Katie?! (*No response.*) Katie?... Katie, can you hear me?!... Are you there?!...

(*A flash of LIGHTNING and a crack of THUNDER. Immediately the gramophone starts to play the Charleston, then the needle scratches back and forth across the record, snatches of the tune emerging at an abnormally high speed. Abruptly it STOPS.*)

LOUISE. (*In a whisper.*) ... Katie?...(*Pause. Then the table THUMPS loudly.*)
BOBBY. My God...
GILLETTE. Be quiet!
LOUISE. ... Katie, is someone with you, dear?... Please answer me. (*A pause, then another loud THUMP.*)

LOUISE. ...Is it ... a man? (*The table begins to shake violently, rising from the floor under their hands.*)

GILLETTE. Press down! Hold it down!

LOUISE. Katie! (*The table falls back to the floor with a BUMP.*)

MARION. Jesus Christ...

LOUISE. ... A woman, to speak with one of us ...? (*Pause. THUMP.*)

GILLETTE. (*In a hoarse whisper.*) Maude?...

LOUISE. ...Is it anyone we know? ... (*No response.*) ... Katie?...Katie, please... (*THUMP.*)

LOUISE. ... Is it ... Is ... is – (*LOUISE begins to gasp. Her gasping becomes violent, tortured. It seems that she can't breathe and is desperately fighting for air—as though she's being strangled. She begins to choke, her throat constricted, in terrible pain.*)

LILLY. Louise!

MAY. Do something!

LEO. For God's sake –

GILLETTE. Leave her alone!

BOBBY. But she can't breathe –

GILLETTE. Do as I say!

(*LOUISE continues to struggle, then suddenly collapses onto the table, face down. Two seconds pass, then, with a loud gasp, her body is thrown upward, so that she's standing, but with her fingers still on the table. Then, quietly at first, a very different voice emerges from her lips. A feminine voice, heavy and sad –.)*

LOUISE. ...May ...May ...May... *(MAY doesn't answer.)*

GILLETTE. *(In a loud voice.)* There is someone named May here.

LOUISE. ...May...Redding...

GILLETTE. There is a May Dison here.

LOUISE. May...

BOBBY. *(To MAY.)* Say something –

LILLY. *(To BOBBY.)* Be quiet –

LOUISE. May...

MAY. ...Who is it?!

LOUISE. Speak to me...

MAY. Who is it!?

LOUISE. *(A singsong, like a nursery rhyme.)* The woosel cock so black of hue, with orange tawny bill, The throstle with his note so true, The wren with little quill–

MAY. Oh no...

LOUISE. The finch, the sparrow and the lark The plain-song cuckoo grey–

MAY. *(A frightened cry.)* MAUDE! ...MAUDE?

LOUISE. Cobweb...Darling Cobweb...

MAY. No...Please...

LOUISE. I love you, May. I miss you...

MAY. Maude...

LOUISE. I didn't want to leave you. Ever...

MAY. Yes. I know. I understand.

LOUISE. You know the truth —
MAY. I do.
LOUISE. I would never leave you...Ever...
MAY. I know that. Maude, I promise —
LOUISE. May —
MAY. I promise —
LOUISE. May... The truth...
MAY. I know...
LOUISE. ...It was murder...*Murder!*
MAY. I *know!* I know... (*Shocked silence.*)
BOBBY. May?...
LEO. God Almighty.
GILLETTE.   (*In   a   loud   voice.*)
Maude?...Maude, it's William.
LOUISE. May...
GILLETTE. Who was it, Maude? Please,for
God's sake. Tell me!
LOUISE. May...
GILLETTE. Can you hear me? Maude —?!

(*Slowly, on the back wall, against the curtains,
     facing MAY, the IMAGE OF A WOMAN's
     HEAD begins to form, larger than life. The
     features become increasingly distinct...*)

BOBBY. (*The first to see it.*) Oh, my God —
LEO. Oh, no...(*They all stare at the image.*)
GILLETTE. Maude, listen to me. You must
tell me.
LOUISE. May... Trust me —
MAY. I do.

LOUISE. Trust me...(*The IMAGE begins to fade. As it does, MAY stands up, as if in a trance.*)

MAY. Stay. Please stay...

LOUISE. I love you...

GILLETTE. Maude.

BOBBY. May – (*MAY moves around the table, toward the fading image –.*)

MAY. Don't go...Please...Maude...MAUDE! (*Her voice rises to a SCREAM. She rushes to the wall, but runs into a table with a lamp and glasses on it. She falls with a loud crash –.*)

MAY. MAUDE!! (*Simultaneously, LOUISE screams and sits bolt upright with a violent jerk.*)

GILLETTE. May! (*He and the others jump from their seats and run to MAY, who lies on the floor, sobbing hysterically.*)

MARION. Turn on the lights!

BOBBY. May!

LILLY. Help her up!

BOBBY. The lights!

MARION. For God's sake!

MAY. Maude! Please! ...

(*GILLETTE runs to the hall door and turns on the LIGHTS. Everyone is huddled around MAY, helping her up.*)

LILLY. It's all right, dear. It's all right.

MAY. Maude...

BOBBY. I've got her.

MARION. Watch the glass –

BOBBY. Are you hurt? –
MARION. Be careful.
GILLETTE. Leo?...
BOBBY. (*To MAY.*) I'm right here...

(*GILLETTE, standing at the door, sees that LEO is lying unconscious across the table, his arms outstretched, his head turned to one side.*)

GILLETTE. Leo! (*As he rushes to him, MARION turns, sees him and screams.*)
MARION. Leo! (*She rushes to him in a panic.*)
LILLY. Oh my God –
MARION. Leo?!...
GILLETTE. (*To BOBBY.*) Get him some brandy!
MARION. Oh, God, no...
LOUISE. (*Starting to focus now.*) Leo?...
GILLETTE. Bobby! –
BOBBY. I'm coming –
MARION. Leo...
MAY. (*To LILLY.*) Is he...
LILLY. Willie?
GILLETTE. He's alive.
LEO. (*Groggy.*) What...what happened...
MARION. Shh. Hold your head up.
LEO. I think I fainted.
GILLETTE. That's an understatement.
MARION. Chest pains?

LEO. Hm-m. ...No.

MARION. Are you sure?

LEO. I'm sure.

LOUISE. (*To MAY.*) Are you cut?

MAY. No. (*She feels her arms.*) No.

BOBBY. (*To LILLY.*) Let's get her upstairs.

MAY. (*Standing.*) I'm really fine...

LILLY. Of course you are.

MAY. Leo?

LEO. I'm fine, dear. Are you all right?

MAY. I guess so.

(*Long pause. Everyone is still for a moment. MAY gazes around the room, deeply troubled.*)

LEO. Maude.

MAY. ...She was my sister.

BOBBY. (*A murmur.*) Good God.

MAY. She was murdered. (*Silence. They all stare at her.*)

GILLETTE. (*Taking control.*) I suggest that we sort this out in the morning. It's late.

BOBBY. (*To MAY.*) He's right. Come on. (*BOBBY and LILLY help MAY to the stairs.*)

GILLETTE. (*To LEO.*) Let's go. You too. You can finish that upstairs. (*The brandy.*)

LEO. Right. (*He gets up, a bit unsteadily.*)

MARION. Hold on. (*She takes his arm. Meanwhile LILLY, MAY and BOBBY head up the stairs.*)

BOBBY. Careful.

MAY. I'm fine.

LILLY. (*To MAY.*) Now it's right to bed... (*They exit, as GILLETTE, LEO and MARION reach the stairs.*)

GILLETTE. Watch the step.

LEO. I'm really quite all right. Not exactly my finest hour.

MARION. Don't be an idiot.

LOUISE. Leo? (*He turns.*) I'm very sorry.

LEO. Hardly your fault. Just the shock, I guess. Maude...

GILLETTE. Yes.

MARION. Come on, dear. (*GILLETTE stays at the foot of the stairs, as MARION and LEO go up.*)

GILLETTE. Can I bring you anything? Tea? More brandy?

LEO. No, no. I'm fine. Just fine...

MARION. (*Badly shaken and angry, pauses on the balcony.*) Next time, William, do me a favor...and leave us out of it.

GILLETTE. (*Chastened.*) Will do.

LEO. Good night.

GILLETTE. Good night.

LOUISE. Good night.

(*LEO and MARION exit. GILLETTE and LOUISE are alone now. He sighs, looks at the debris on the floor. LOUISE walks to the bar and pours out two drinks. Long pause. Finally —*)

LOUISE. Satisfactory?

GILLETTE. Oh, yes. Well done. (*He presses a button on the underside of the table, where LOUISE was sitting. The IMAGE OF MAUDE appears on the wall. He lets his finger up and the IMAGE FADES. She hands him his drink.*) I thought we'd agreed that Maude and I would exchange a few ...choice words.

LOUISE. Yes...

GILLETTE. But.

LOUISE. (*Troubled.*) It didn't seem right somehow. It—it didn't fit. I don't know why. I'm sorry.

GILLETTE. Not at all. It couldn't have gone better. You even sounded like her.

LOUISE. That's what you wanted.

GILLETTE. Oh, absolutely. (*He looks at her curiously.*) You're not upset?

LOUISE. No. Of course not. (*Pause.*) Just...angry, I suppose. If you're right.

GILLETTE. Oh, it was murder. I assure you of that.

LOUISE. (*Puts down her glass.*) I'll do anything, William. *Anything* to avenge her. You know that.

GILLETTE. Yes, I know. (*Pause.*)

LOUISE. (*Quietly.*) Hold me –?

GILLETTE. Sorry?

LOUISE. I asked ... if you would hold me.

GILLETTE. ... Certainly. (*He puts down his glass and goes to her. She puts her hands on the back of his neck, finds his lips and kisses him fiercely, hungrily. As she's kissing him, MAY suddenly hurries onto the balcony, about to say something—but she sees them and stops dead. She stares at them, frozen, in shock. A flash of LIGHTNING, THUNDER. The LIGHTS fade.*)

End of Scene.

Scene 3

A half hour later.
As the LIGHTS come up the French doors are wide open and the broken glass from the last scene has been cleared away. GILLETTE, alone, is standing on the threshold of the terrace, facing the darkness outside. He wears trousers, shirt, slippers, and a patterned silk dressing gown— much the same outfit that Holmes wears when at leisure in Baker Street.
The storm has passed now and all is quiet. GILLETTE takes a deep breath of the clean air and contemplates the stillness for a time. His reverie is interrupted when the hall door opens and LILLY enters, wearing a nightgown and carrying a glass of milk.

LILLY. I thought you'd be up.

GILLETTE. Did you get her to bed?

LILLY. Yes, the poor thing. She was terribly shaken. I hope there was a good reason for all that nonsense.

GILLETTE. Nonsense? My dear, you sat here in the shadow of death —

LILLY. Oh don't play cat and mouse with me. I didn't change your filthy diapers for nothing...

GILLETTE. (*Laughing.*) You sweetheart.

LILLY. And poor Leo. He almost gave *me* a heart attack.

GILLETTE. Yes, that was odd, wasn't it.

LILLY. Odd? It wasn't odd at all. The poor man was frightened. We all were.

GILLETTE. Mm.

LILLY. I still can't get over it. May and Maude. I can see it now, around the eyes. You knew all about it, of course.

GILLETTE. No, no. I suspected it, that's all.

LILLY. So you frightened the poor girl out of her wits.

GILLETTE. Well she wasn't about to tell me. She's had the past three months to do that.

LILLY. You could have asked her.

GILLETTE. And she would have denied it! Lilly, I had to know.

LILLY. Did you?

GILLETTE. Yes. (*Pause.*)

LILLY. Willie...If Maude was murdered—and I don't believe it, not for a second—but if she was...I think you should stay out of it.

GILLETTE. Just forget about it?

LILLY. Yes. Please.

GILLETTE. All right, dear. If you say so.

LILLY. Willie...

GILLETTE. I'll think about it. (*Pause.*)

LILLY. (*Sighing as she closes the French doors.*) You'd think out here at least we could have a little peace and quiet.

GILLETTE. "It is my firm belief, Watson, that the lowest and vilest alleys in London do not present a more dreadful record of sin than does the smiling and beautiful countryside." The Adventures of the Copper Beeches.

LILLY. All right, Mr. Holmes, let's get you to bed.

GILLETTE. I'm tired, Aunt Lilly.

LILLY. Of course you are, dear. Let's go. (*She turns out one of the LIGHTS.*)

GILLETTE. Not just yet. You go ahead.

LILLY. Oh Willie –

GILLETTE. I'll be up in a minute. (*He sits in one of the armchairs and leans his head back.*)

LILLY. (*Hesitates, but realizes that it's a losing battle.*) All right. But keep warm. (*She adjusts his dressing gown over his knees, then kisses him on the cheek.*)

GILLETTE. (*Dreamily.*) Maude loved this house, you know.

LILLY. I know.

GILLETTE. It tickled her no end.

LILLY. (*Sitting next to him, on the arm of the chair.*) Maude is gone, Willie. It's no good, living in the past. You really must let her go.

GILLETTE. How can I?

LILLY. I don't want you to be lonely, dearest.

GILLETTE. With you here? Impossible.

LILLY. I'm not immortal.

GILLETTE. Wrong, wrong. That's just what you are.

LILLY. Willie ...

GILLETTE. All right. (*He leans his head back, sadly.*)

LILLY. She would have wanted you to find someone else. I promise.

GILLETTE. Some else...Shall I flip a coin? Advertise?

LILLY. Oh, you could have a hundred women. I used to trip over them, waiting backstage for a glimpse of you. Dying for your autograph.

GILLETTE. Perhaps I should propose in writing. "Please marry me, and best of luck. William Gillette."

LILLY. (*Ignoring him.*) You should get to know someone. Take her to dinner. Go dancing.

GILLETTE. (*Bored.*) Yes, dear.

LILLY. If it matters, and I don't suppose it does, I do think that May couldn't be lovelier.

GILLETTE. May? (*He stares at her and laughs.*) May?!...First of all I could be her father—

LILLY. You need a younger woman.

GILLETTE. And what about Bobby? She's never without him.

LILLY. Oh you're such an idiot. She'd give up ten Bobbys for you, like that.

GILLETTE. Lilly...

LILLY. The girl positively dotes on you.

GILLETTE. My dear, it may well be that she respects me, as an actor...

LILLY. (*Standing.*) Oh, please, you're so unnerving. You give me a headache.

GILLETTE. All right, all right. Tomorrow, first thing after breakfast, I'll take her for a walk and ravish her.

LILLY. And I'm sure it would do you both a world of good. I'm going to bed. (*She walks to the stairs and turns.*)

LILLY. Don't be long.

GILLETTE. I won't. (*She goes up the stairs.*) Good night, dearest.

LILLY. Good night, my love. (*She exits.*)

(*He watches her disappear. Then he sighs and looks sadly around the room. Finally he nestles down into the chair and stares into space, thinking. Thinking...The LIGHTS fade to complete darkness. THE LIGHTS REMAIN LOWERED FOR SEVERAL*

*SECONDS TO DENOTE THE PASSING OF
ONE HOUR.)*

*(When the LIGHTS come up, the room is dark and
empty. GILLETTE is gone. The CLOCK in the
hall, off right, chimes three o'clock. A
moment later, MAY enters on the balcony.
She is still dressed, despite the hour. With
only the MOONLIGHT shining through the
French doors, she's barely visible. She looks
down at the room to make certain that no one
is there, then moves silently down the stairs
and into the room. She turns on one of the
lamps; then she opens her purse and pulls out
her gun. She looks at it, deliberating. It feels
cold and alien to her. She makes up her mind,
tucks her purse under her arm and walks to
the hall door. She opens it to leave...and stops
dead with a frightened gasp.)*

MAY. No! (*She backs away, frightened,
staring into the hall, hiding her gun.*)
Please!...What do you want?! (*Pause. Then
GILLETTE appears in the doorway.*)
GILLETTE. What are you doing here?
MAY. Nothing...
GILLETTE. (*Approaching her.*) What the hell
are you doing –?!
MAY. Hold it! (*She whips the gun from behind
her back and holds it with both hands, aimed
directly at him. Her hands are shaking.*)

MAY. Just ... stay there.

GILLETTE. Oh, for God's sake –

MAY. Stay where you are! Don't move.

GILLETTE. May ...

MAY. I'm leaving here ... right now... and I don't want any trouble. All right? ... (*No answer.*) All right?!

GILLETTE. But if I try to stop you, you'll shoot me. Is that the idea?

MAY. Yes.

GILLETTE. Well I admire your conviction, my dear, but I doubt if you'll do it.

MAY. You'd be surprised.

GILLETTE. You're right, I would. I filled your gun with blanks this evening, after I found it in your handbag.

MAY. ...You're lying.

GILLETTE. Besides, you couldn't fire it anyway without releasing the safety catch. That little thing near your thumb.

(*MAY automatically looks to where he's indicated, turning the gun as she does so. The instant the gun is turned, GILLETTE grabs her wrist. They struggle.*)

MAY. (*Struggling.*) You ...bastard!

(*He squeezes her wrist like a vise, and she drops the gun to the floor. Then he shoves her roughly away.*)

MAY. *Bastard!*

GILLETTE. (*He picks up the gun.*) For your future information, the Smith and Wesson .32 doesn't have a safety catch. (*He puts the gun on the table next to his chair. As he does, she jumps at him, arms outstretched, enraged. They struggle again, more violently, until GILLETTE knocks her to the floor. For a moment, she's stunned by the blow. Angry.*) Now sit down! There. (*The sofa.*)

MAY. I hate you.

GILLETTE. Yes, I can see that. Now what the hell is going on!?

MAY. Nothing.

GILLETTE. (*Approaching her.*) May —

MAY. (*Panicked.*) Get away from me!...Please I—I want to leave here. Now. *Please!* (*Pause.*)

GILLETTE. I'm afraid I can't allow that.

MAY. ...That's what I thought.

GILLETTE. Did you? Now why is that? (*No answer.*) May, answer me — !

MAY. What do you think!? ...Murderer. (*Silence.*)

GILLETTE. I beg your pardon.

MAY. You murdered Maude. You thought I didn't know.

GILLETTE. (*Quietly.*) Either you're very confused, my dear, or you're very mad.

MAY. There's no use denying it. She told me.

GILLETTE. May, your sister is dead.

MAY. She wrote me a letter.

GILLETTE. From the other side?

MAY. Stop it! I know what you did! I know how you were jealous, and — and threatened her. And killed her. She told me everything!

GILLETTE. In a letter.

MAY. Yes! (*Defiantly, she pulls a letter from her pocket.*) Surprised?

GILLETTE. That depends on what it says. Why don't you read it to me.

MAY. Read it yourself. (*She tosses it on the table.*)

GILLETTE. (*He picks up the letter, a single sheet, and glances curiously at both sides. As he begins to read it, MAY turns away. Reading.*) "April 11, 1921. My darling Cobweb...My life is in danger, and I am leaving here tonight, forever. I will get in touch with you as soon as I can, when I know it's safe...Love has turned to jealousy, and jealousy to hatred. If something happens, and if, by any chance, you ever learn the truth, I pray to God that you'll understand and forgive me. Ever in memory. Maude." (*During the following, he scrutinizes the letter through the light of the lamp.*) How did you get this?

MAY. Oh stop it!

GILLETTE. How did you get it?! Was it through the mail?

MAY. Yes!

GILLETTE. When?

MAY. The day ... the day after she died.

GILLETTE. Do you have the envelope?

MAY. I hate you.

GILLETTE. Do you have it!

MAY. No! I—I threw it out.

GILLETTE. It looks like her handwriting...

MAY. Of course it is!

GILLETTE. "Love has turned to jealousy, and jealousy to hatred." I can see at least why you suspected me. I loved her.

MAY. Did you? The way you love Louise? (*He looks at her, surprised.*) I saw you, kissing her!

GILLETTE. That's none of your business.

MAY. And what about the seance! You made a—a joke of Maude! You both did!

GILLETTE. My dear –

MAY. You did! –

GILLETTE. It was not a joke! For God's sake!...(*He turns away to calm himself. Quietly.*) May...I loved your sister more than you will ever understand.

(*MAY stiffens visibly at this obvious slight.*)

GILLETTE. That night...she was frightened of something, in a panic, she wanted to leave here at once. She wouldn't tell me what it was, but I insisted on going with her. I left her alone for...five minutes. I was in the bedroom, changing, when I heard the shot. (*Pause.*) I knew that she was murdered from the moment I found her. If she'd wanted to kill herself, she could have done it anywhere. But she was dressed, she came down here...she was scared to death.

MAY. What about the police?

GILLETTE. They couldn't have cared less. As far as they were concerned, it was cut and dried. She owned a gun, it was in her hand, no signs of a struggle...The point is, I couldn't prove anything. I had no evidence. No clues, no motives, nothing! (*Pause.*) Then you came along. An unknown actress, you auditioned for the part...and at certain moments, when you turned your head and looked at me, you were remarkably like her. I had a lead, you see. Finally!

MAY. I don't believe you.

GILLETTE. May –

MAY. Why should I!? Give me one good reason.

GILLETTE. ...All right, I will. (*He walks to the desk. Turning his back on her, he opens a drawer and begins rummaging through it. As he continues his search, MAY watches him, then sees her gun on the table, where GILLETTE left it. Without a sound, she moves to the table, picks up the gun and points it at his back. Without turning around-*) I told you I put blanks in it, so why don't you put it down. (*He turns, holding the letter, which he scans quickly.*) Good. I'll trade you. (*Without resistance, he takes the gun and hands her the letter. She eyes him curiously. He puts the gun back on the table.*) She left it for me the night she was murdered. I found it later, on the table. It's in her handwriting, you notice.

MAY. ...Yes.

GILLETTE. Read it.

MAY. (*After a pause, her voice shaky.*) "April 11...My dearest William...I must leave you now, I have no choice. I cannot bear to say good-bye...because I love you...more than life itself...My heart is ... breaking..." (*Her voice trails away. She stands, without moving, reading the rest of it to herself.*)

GILLETTE. Well?

(*She grits her teeth. She is trying desperately not to cry. She folds the note, puts it down and turns away. Her shoulders begin to shake. She starts to cry, softly at first, then starts to sob bitterly. GILLETTE goes to her and she clutches onto him, her head on his shoulder.*)

MAY. (*Through her tears.*) I'm sorry...

GILLETTE. Shh...It's all right. You've had a lot of shocks today, that's all.

MAY. I'm sorry.

GILLETTE. I'm sorry, too. About this evening. I meant to find out about you, but I didn't mean to scare you to death.

MAY. (*Hoarsely.*) It's all right...I should have just...shown you the letter, I guess, but at first... I thought it was you... And then, after a few weeks, I didn't think so, and then tonight, after what happened, I thought it must be you. And I was so frightened!

GILLETTE. You must have loved her very much.

MAY. But why?! I don't understand it! Why would anyone do such a thing?!

GILLETTE. Jealousy. Hatred. You read the letter.

MAY. (*Standing, then moving around the room*) I suppose it could have been anyone, really. Someone we don't even know about. He could have followed her here, from New York. I mean, he could have called her that day, and then arranged to meet her and then...then killed her.

(*But GILLETTE isn't listening. Something has distracted him. During MAY's speech, he walks to the desk and opens the top drawer.*)

MAY. ...Right?

GILLETTE. (*He pulls a gun, his own, from the drawer and turns, pointing it straight at her.*) Wrong. (*She sees the gun and starts.*)

GILLETTE. Now don't move.

MAY. No...

GILLETTE. Be quiet.

MAY. No —!

GILLETTE. Be still!

(*She freezes. He listens intently for something, then says evenly —*)

GILLETTE. Now listen to me. I want you to act very natural, and move away from the window.

MAY. (*Understanding now, glancing backward.*) Oh. Do you think someone's —

GILLETTE. (*Urgently.*) Move.

(*She walks quickly away from the windows and stops. After several seconds without a sound, GILLETTE advances slowly to one side of the French doors. He peers through the windows to the terrace. Several more seconds pass, and GILLETTE sighs.*)

MAY. (*Advancing.*) Was someone listening?

GILLETTE. Well if he was, he's certainly —

(*A GUNSHOT explodes, shattering a window. GILLETTE, hit, spins, but stays on his feet. MAY screams and runs to him.*)

GILLETTE. Get down! (*He leaps straight at her, taking her to the floor—as two more GUNSHOTS explode, shattering two more windows and one of the wall lamps.*)

MAY. My God!

GILLETTE. (*He is on top of MAY, pinning her to the floor.*) Are you all —

MAY. You're bleeding!

GILLETTE. Are you all right?

MAY. Yes!

GILLETTE. Stay here! (*He struggles across the floor to his gun, which he dropped when hit. We see now that his left arm is covered with blood. He reaches the gun, grabs it and struggles to his feet.*)

MAY. Don't —

(*He pauses for a second, then jumps in front of the door, firing a shot as he goes. He flings open the doors and fires two more shots in quick succession. At this moment we hear LILLY's voice upstairs. "Willie! ...Willie?!"*)

GILLETTE. (*Turning back into the room.*) No good. (*He stumbles, dropping the gun. MAY springs up to catch him, but he falls to his knees.*)

MAY. Oh no.

GILLETTE. (*In pain.*) I'm all right...

LILLY. (*Rushes down the stairs.*) Willie!

MAY. Call a doctor! He's bleeding!

LILLY. God almighty!

GILLETTE. (*Overlapping.*) Stupid... (*He falls to the floor.*)

MAY. Please, call a doctor!

(*LILLY hurries to the phone.*)

GILLETTE. (*Struggling to get up.*) Just my arm...

MAY. Lie still!

GILLETTE. I'm fine –
MAY. Don't talk!
LILLY. (*On the phone.*) Hello...hello...Greta! It's Lilly Warner. We need an ambulance at the Castle, right away –
MAY. (*Overlapping "Greta"*) And tell them to hurry!
GILLETTE. (*On his knees, overlapping "We need".*) I'm fine...
MAY. Shhh. Don't talk. You'll be all right...
LILLY. (*Overlapping.*) Yes, he's been shot.

(*With a groan, GILLETTE falls back onto the floor, unconscious.*)

MAY. (*Holding his head.*) No!
LILLY. Right. (*She hangs up and turns.*) Fifteen minutes.

(*Tableau. The LIGHTS fade to BLACKOUT.*)

End of Act I

ACT II

Scene 1

The following evening, about 6:15.

The last of the day's SUNLIGHT streams in through the windows. BOBBY, in evening dress, his tie undone, is alone in the room, sitting inert in the large armchair, facing front. Next to the chair, on the floor, lie three issues of Variety. *BOBBY's eyes are closed, his mouth hangs open and his head droops, motionless, on his chest. One of his arms juts from his body at rather a peculiar angle. He may be asleep; but then again he may be dead. The more we look at him, the more we realize that he isn't breathing. Or at least he doesn't appear to be.*

After a few seconds, the door to the hall opens and LILLY appears, carrying a tray with an ice bucket and a pitcher of tomato juice. She looks tired. She closes the door behind her with her foot, and it slams rather loudly. BOBBY doesn't move. She crosses the room, walking behind the armchair, and places the tray on the sideboard. She hasn't spotted BOBBY yet, but she may at any moment. She opens the bar and sets out a few glasses; she puts tongs in the ice bucket and stirs

*the ice. In fact, she's making quite a racket.
BOBBY's body, however, doesn't move a hair.*

*LILLY finishes setting up the bar and sighs.
The sigh turns into a noisy yawn, which she
covers with her hand. She looks at her watch and
realizes that it's late. Then she turns—again
missing BOBBY's presence—and hurries up the
stairs.*

*Several seconds pass; then MAY appears
descending the stairs. She, too, looks tired. When
she reaches the floor, she tosses her purse onto the
sofa, then notices the bar. With her back to the
body, she fills a glass with ice and tomato juice—
then stirs it with a spoon. All pretty noisy. She
takes a sip, sighs, and walks toward the sofa.
Then she sees BOBBY. She smiles. Just like
BOBBY to fall asleep in the living room.*

MAY. (*Gently.*) Bobby. (*No reply. A little
louder* –) ...Bobby...? (*No reply. MAY's face
begins to change. Shaking slightly, she puts her
glass on a table. Louder still.*) Bobby?...(*She
hesitates, frightened, then rushes to him. A half-
scream* –) Bobby!

BOBBY. AHH!

MAY. (*Simultaneously, a scream.*) AHH!

BOBBY. (*Jumping up.*) What's the matter?!

MAY. Bobby...

BOBBY. What is it?! What happened?!

MAY. (*Overlapping.*) Ohh...I thought...I
thought....

BOBBY. WHAT HAPPENED!!??

MAY. Nothing happened! Ohh...You didn't move...and I ...I thought you were dead!

BOBBY. (*Recovering.*) No. No, I don't think so.

MAY. I mean...you looked...dead.

BOBBY. Thanks a lot.

MAY. Not now.

BOBBY. Well that's a relief.

MAY. Ohh...(*She sits.*)

BOBBY. I was having this nightmare. We were onstage, the bit in Act Three, at the gas works, when Holmes lets you out of the closet. Well instead of being scared, you calmly opened your purse, pulled out a revolver and shot me three times. Real bullets.

MAY. Oh, please...

BOBBY. The audience gave you a standing ovation.

MAY. You made that up.

BOBBY. (*Unhappily.*) No, I didn't. I remember thinking as I fell: "Damn. No curtain call."

MAY. Oh don't be gruesome.

BOBBY. Drink?

MAY. I have one.

(*BOBBY potters to the bar and makes himself a drink.*)

MAY. (*Yawning.*) Ohhh. It must be four o'clock.

BOBBY. (*Looks at his watch.*) It's after six.

MAY. Oh, my God. I guess I was tired.

BOBBY. (*Acidly.*) I guess so.

MAY. Have the police all gone?

BOBBY. Mm. Hours ago. And a more unsmiling lot I've never seen. No wonder I had nightmares.

MAY. Have you seen William?

BOBBY. "William?" Yes, of course. "William." He went along to the police station. To fill out a complaint or something.

MAY. I hope he's all right.

BOBBY. I'm sure you do.

MAY. Bobby, he lost a lot of blood.

BOBBY. Mm. Buckets.

MAY. He did. He could have been killed.

BOBBY. Well he wasn't. He got a flesh wound. Big deal. I've had worse mosquito bites.

MAY. You didn't see it. It was horrible.

BOBBY. I wonder what you'd say if I got shot. "Dumb bugger. Shoulda ducked."

MAY. Bobby.

BOBBY. All right, all right! He got shot in the arm and my heart bleeds for him. (*Beat.*) Medical mystery.

MAY. (*Ignores him.*) Here. (*She extends her glass.*) Juice.

BOBBY. (*Taking her glass.*) One tomato juice for Miss May...Redding. (*No reply.*) You certainly had us all fooled, you know.

MAY. Did I?

BOBBY. Well me, at least. You wouldn't want to tell me why, I suppose...

MAY. No. I wouldn't.

BOBBY. Right. (*He goes to the bar and pours her a glass of tomato juice. Eyeing the juice as it streams from the pitcher into her glass.*) He did lose a lot of blood. (*He brings her the juice.*)

MAY. (*Preoccupied.*) Bobby...?

BOBBY. Mm?

MAY. Do you believe that Maude was murdered?

BOBBY. Well you said so. Last night.

MAY. Yes, I know. I mean, I thought so, but it doesn't make sense anymore. There was no reason. No motive.

BOBBY. No motive? My God, the place is crawling with 'em. Everybody's got a motive. That's the trouble.

MAY. Who?

BOBBY. (*Ticking them off.*) Leo, tired of playing second banana, wreaks his revenge. Marion, jealous of Maude's looks and talent since the day she auditioned. Lilly, terrified of losing her darling boy. Gillette himself, if Maude didn't want him after all, and God knows how she could...And you.

MAY. Me?

BOBBY. Well, you have admitted you were sisters. After lying about it for three months.

MAY. So?

BOBBY. So...who inherited Maude's estate?

MAY. She didn't have an estate. Not much, anyway.

BOBBY. According to you.

MAY. I was in Cleveland when it happened —

BOBBY. According to you —

MAY. Oh stop it! Don't be an ass.

BOBBY. I'm not saying you did it. I was merely demonstrating that you had a motive.

MAY. Well, big deal. So did you.

BOBBY. Oh, absolutely. Top of the list. Assuming, of course...that I loved her. (*Pause.*) After that, it's clear sailing. I couldn't bear to see Gillette slobbering all over her, so in a fit of jealousy I shot her. Through the head. I would have strangled her, but she might have screamed.

(*MAY turns and looks at him.*)

BOBBY. So...when Gillette finally got on to me—and it certainly took him long enough—well, naturally I tried to kill him. (*Pause.*) Dead of night. Bobby Carlyle steals down the back stairs and onto the terrace. He waits in the darkness, racked with jealousy. Then, at last, a shadow at the window. A flicker of life. Slowly, he draws out his .38 caliber, single-action

Remington. Pcchh! Pcchh! Unfortunately, I only winged him. (*Pause.*)

MAY. (*Cold, angry.*) You don't care at all, do you? About anything.

BOBBY. (*Quietly.*) Wrong. I care about a lot of things. I care, for instance, that you were down here at 3 A.M. With him.

MAY. I explained that.

BOBBY. You came down for some milk. You were thirsty.

MAY. You don't understand.

BOBBY. Fine. Tell me. Go ahead.

MAY. Nothing happened —

BOBBY. Alone together at 3 in the morning. Was it on the sofa, or just the rug —?

MAY. (*Flaring up.*) Bobby, stop it! You've got it all wrong.

BOBBY. Like hell I do. He's twice your age, for God's sake. More.

MAY. But nothing happened —

BOBBY. (*Working himself up.*) Every time I turn around, there he is, cutting in again —

MAY. That's not fair —

BOBBY. And he's the hero, of course. Star of the show, the great Holmes —

MAY. Bobby, listen —

BOBBY. Well I've had it! First it was Maude, now it's you.

MAY. Leave her out of this!

BOBBY. It's true!

MAY. You're being stupid!

BOBBY. I have just ... had it!!!

(*In a sudden fit of violence, he hurls his glass to the floor, shattering it. Dead silence. MAY stares at him, frightened and angry. He stares back. Abruptly, she turns away and runs up the stairs.*)

BOBBY. May...(*He hurries to the stairs.*) May, wait! (*But it's too late. She's gone. He looks up the stairs, turns at last and sighs deeply, pulling himself together. Pause. He looks at the broken glass, realizing that he'll have to clean it up.*) ...Shit. (*He stoops down and begins picking up the pieces, when MARION appears on the stairs, her eyes blazing. She's in a robe, but her face and hair are done up for the party.*)
MARION. Bitch!
BOBBY. Sorry?
MARION. I said she's a bitch. (*She heads straight to the bar.*)
BOBBY. Ah. Louise. (*He deposits the broken glass in a waste basket.*)
MARION. She follows him around like a goddamned bloodhound.
LEO. (*Off.*) Marion! (*She turns to the bar and pours out a stiff one, as LEO enters on the balcony. He's partly dressed, in tuxedo pants and a shirt unbuttoned down the front.*) Marion! Will you get the hell up here! (*No answer.*) She borrowed a comb, for God's sake. A stupid comb.

MARION. While I happened to be out.

LEO. She didn't know that.

MARION. How very convenient.

LEO. What's the matter with you!?

MARION. With me? The bastard feels guilty and he blames me.

LEO. I do not feel guilty!

MARION. Boy, are you a lousy liar!

LEO. MARION, YOU'RE MAKING A SCENE!...Now get upstairs!

MARION. When I'm good and ready. (*She turns back to the bar and ignores him. LEO stares at her, ready to burst; then he draws himself up, turns on his heel and exits without a word. Pause. MARION walks to the sofa and sits down heavily. BOBBY watches her. She looks miserable.*)

BOBBY. You may be overreacting, you know. People do that.

MARION. She's been flirting with him since she walked in that door. Her and her ectoplasm. (*Pause.*) Get me a drink.

BOBBY. You have one.

MARION. (*Drains her glass.*) Get me another one. (*He takes her glass and goes to the bar. MARION leans back and sighs heavily.*)

BOBBY. Marion...

MARION. (*Numb.*) Yes, dear.

BOBBY. If it's any consolation...I think she did it. Louise.

MARION. Did what?

BOBBY. Shot Gillette. Tried to murder him.

MARION. (*Beat. MARION smiles.*) Oh good. Maybe they'll hang her.

BOBBY. Listen. I'm serious... (*He looks around to make sure that all the doors are closed. Galvanized, conspiratorially.*) Now look. Last night, after the shooting, who was the last one down the stairs? Hm?

MARION. (*Thinks.*) You were.

BOBBY. Besides me! Just in front of me.

MARION. ...Louise.

BOBBY. Right. Why? Because it took her that long to run up the back stairs, change into her slippers and come down here.

MARION. It took you even longer.

BOBBY. (*Sighs with disgust.*) Because I happen to sleep in the buff. It took me five minutes to find a robe. I was running around up there like the Keystone Kops.

MARION. Maybe she sleeps in the buff, too. She would.

BOBBY. All right, forget that. But look at it this way. Process of elimination. I didn't shoot him...

MARION. You're sure?

BOBBY. Marion...

MARION. Fine. (*At this moment, LOUISE appears on the balcony. Like MARION, she's done up for the party, but wears a robe. Neither BOBBY nor MARION realizes that she's entered. She stops and listens, as BOBBY continues talking to MARION.*)

BOBBY. Now May couldn't have, she was down here with him. And we can forget about Lilly. So who's left? You and Leo have the perfect alibi. You were sleeping together when it happened. Right? ...

MARION. ...Right.

BOBBY. Well? Voila. Louise did it. She had to.

LOUISE. Louise did what?

(*BOBBY freezes, then turns. MARION stands. Dead silence.*)

BOBBY. Shot Gillette.

LOUISE. Did I? How extremely clever of me. (*She descends the stairs.*) Did I have a motive? Or was it just target practice?

BOBBY. I'm working on it.

LOUISE. Good for you. (*She retrieves her cigarette case from one of the tables.*) And incidentally...you might ask Marion about that perfect alibi of hers. Because Leo wasn't sleeping with her when it happened. Was he, dear?

(*MARION stares at LOUISE but says nothing. Then, without warning, she slaps LOUISE hard across the face. Stunned silence, broken suddenly by LILLY's voice from upstairs.*)

LILLY. (*Off.*) Marion!? (*LILLY enters down the stairs. She's wearing her party dress, but*

holding it up in front. She's in a state.)
...Marion!...(*She sees LOUISE.*) Oh hello, dear.
You'd better hurry. It's getting late, you know.

LOUISE. Yes, I'll be right down. (*She glances
at MARION, then exits quickly up the stairs.*)

LILLY. Bobby. Turn around!

BOBBY. Right. (*He does.*)

LILLY. Marion...I'm stuck. (*She turns and
shows MARION the back of her dress, which is
unhooked to the waist.*)

MARION. (*Still in a daze.*) I'll fix it.

LILLY. I can't even get out of the damn thing!

BOBBY. (*Who has turned around again, to
MARION.*) You hold the dress, I'll pull her feet.

LILLY. Oh shut up.

MARION. Come on. (*They head across the
room and up the stairs.*)

LILLY. We're going to be late. I can tell
already ... I should have started earlier. I always
do this. And I just hate being late...(*BOBBY and
MARION exchange a final glance. Then
MARION follows LILLY off.*)

(*BOBBY watches them exit, then wanders to the
sofa to finish his drink. He sits down and
sighs, thinking deeply about the past few
minutes. After a moment, he notices MAY's
purse, which she forgot to take with her. He
looks at it curiously, then remembers the
incident last night—the gun he found in her
purse. The same purse. A look of cunning*

enters his eyes. He glances at the terrace, which is empty, then at both doors, which are closed. He's alone.

He opens the purse. The gun is there. He pulls it out and looks at it thoughtfully. He examines it, turning it over in his hands. Then he smells it, to find out if it's been fired recently. He can't tell. He points it at his nose and grimaces. He's about to put it back, when he notices something else in the purse that makes him curious. He puts the gun on the coffee table, then pulls a letter from the purse [the letter from Act I, Scene 3]. He looks at it skeptically and unfolds it. He starts to read it. He gets as far as the first sentence, when the front door slams, off right. He jerks up, hesitates about what to do—then snaps the purse shut and shoves the letter into the breast pocket of his coat. He stands up and moves away from the table, striking a nonchalant pose...when he sees the gun on the coffee table where he left it. He dashes to it, shoves it into the purse and springs away, once again assuming an air of studied nonchalance. At that moment, the door to the front hall opens, and GILLETTE strides in. He wears a tweed suit and a traveling cape. His left arm is in a sling.)

GILLETTE. (*Removing his cape.*) Well, good evening. Have you managed to catch our "mad gunman" yet? Or is he still haunting the tangled woodlands high above the Connecticut River?

BOBBY. Me?

GILLETTE. Now surely you've been doing something more than dozing in that chair all afternoon, reading *Variety*.

BOBBY. Well, no ...not exactly. How did you, uh...?

GILLETTE. Your face is creased, your fingers have newsprint all over them, and that (*Nodding to the floor –*) is *Variety*. (*He tosses his cape on the sofa and goes to the bar, where he pours himself a glass of tomato juice.*)

BOBBY. I see. Not bad...

LEO. (*Enters at the balcony and comes down the stairs. He's dressed now, in black tie.*) I thought I heard you. How's the arm?

GILLETTE. On the mend. A bit stiff.

LEO. You're lucky it's there at all.

BOBBY. (*To LEO.*) Did you kiss and make up?

LEO. Mind you own damn business.

BOBBY. Well, we're all certainly in a good mood this evening.

LEO. What the hell do you expect!

BOBBY. Sorry. (*He ambles to the mirror and ties his tie.*)

GILLETTE. (*To LEO.*) Trouble in paradise?

LEO. (*False bravado.*) Let's just say the waters are a bit choppy, but the storm is passing.

GILLETTE. Marriage.

LEO. Right. "Makes man and wife one flesh, but leaves 'em still two fools."

GILLETTE. ...Sheridan?

LEO. Congreve. Ha!

GILLETTE. Not my day.

LEO. (*Goes to the bar.*) Any progress? With the police?

GILLETTE. None. Their strategy appears to be that if I get out of their jurisdiction and make it back to New York alive, then with any luck I'll be murdered there.

LEO. Gillette. You don't really believe it was someone here, do you? I mean one of us.

GILLETTE. (*Lounging on the sofa.*) Oh, absolutely. There's no question about it.

LEO. Well, I don't. Not for a second.

BOBBY. Oh, come on. I mean you may not like it, but it's pretty obvious that somebody in this house is a killer.

LEO. Not to me. Just the opposite. It's a question of logic. Look, if somebody here really wanted to kill him, then logically they would try it anyplace but here. They'd wait, then do it elsewhere. So much safer.

GILLETTE. Exactly. Exactly right. That is the key to everything.

LEO. There. You see.

BOBBY. (*To GILLETTE.*) You agree with him?

GILLETTE. I agree that any other reasoning is totally illogical. His conclusion, of course, is totally wrong.

(*LEO and BOBBY glance at each other.*)

GILLETTE. I will admit that for a time I was fooled. The disguise, of course, is extremely clever.

LEO. Gillette, are you feeling all right?

BOBBY. What disguise?

GILLETTE. The disguise being worn by the killer at this very instant. (*Pause. At this moment, LOUISE appears on the stairs and pauses on the landing. An "entrance." She's dressed for the party, gloriously, in a seductive gown.*)

LEO. Louise! (*All eyes turn to her. Beat.*)

LOUISE. Did I miss a button?

LEO. Louise, you look gorgeous.

LOUISE. (*Descending.*) I'll bet you say that to all the girls.

BOBBY. He does. (*LEO gives him a look.*) Now she'll tell us that it's some old rag she found in her suitcase.

LOUISE. On the contrary, I bought it Friday, just for tonight. One does not meet the Great Sarah every day.

GILLETTE. I hope you won't be disappointed, my dear. She's almost eighty, you know.

LOUISE. You have no heart, William. None at all. You'll look at her hands and see an old woman. I shall look in her eyes and see Medea, Camille, Hamlet.

BOBBY. I just hope we get to talk to her. I'll bet they have hordes of people there.

LEO. Over a hundred. That's what I heard.

BOBBY. (*To LOUISE.*) My God, just think of the seance you could have. All those people in one room, holding hands. You could raise the Titanic. (*A deadly pause. LOUISE is not amused.*) Figure of speech.

GILLETTE. Perhaps, young Robert, you'd like to go play some billiards.

BOBBY. Hm? Well that's a thought. Leo?

LEO. Yes, why don't we. (*LEO and BOBBY head to the door, left.*) I could always use a few extra dollars.

BOBBY. (*To GILLETTE and LOUISE.*) Sorry. (*They exit.*)

(*As soon as the door is closed, GILLETTE springs up. He strides to the door and listens, then glances at the terrace and balcony. His manner is urgent now, no nonsense.*)

GILLETTE. All right, what happened?

LOUISE. Not much, I'm afraid. He just sat around all day, reading.

GILLETTE. No little strolls in the woods –?

LOUISE. No, I'm positive.

GILLETTE. Did he make any calls?

LOUISE. Yes, one. About four o'clock.

GILLETTE. And?

LOUISE. ...I couldn't hear him.

GILLETTE. Damn!

LOUISE. I'm sorry. I tried. Did you get to his suitcase?

GILLETTE. Hm? No, I didn't bother. The police found the gun this afternoon.

LOUISE. Where?

GILLETTE. In the bushes out back. He must have thrown it there, after the shooting.

LOUISE. Fingerprints?

GILLETTE. He's not a fool.

LOUISE. Do you think he knows? That you're on to him.

GILLETTE. (*A gleam in his eyes.*) Oh yes, he knows. I made sure of that.

LOUISE. William.You could be wrong.

GILLETTE. I could be...but I'm not. (*Pause.*) Exclude the impossible, and whatever remains, however improbable ...

LOUISE. – must be the truth.

GILLETTE. (*Mildly surprised.*) So...you read Conan Doyle.

LOUISE. How do you think I survived the hospital?

GILLETTE. I thought it might be thinking of me. (*Pause. She smiles at him.*)

LOUISE. That too.

(*At this moment, MAY enters, hurrying down the stairs. She's dressed for the party, but in her bare feet. When she sees GILLETTE and LOUISE together, she stops, sensing their intimacy.*)

GILLETTE. May –
MAY. I...I came down for my purse.
GILLETTE. You look lovely.
MAY. How are you feeling?
GILLETTE. Much better. A thousand times.
MAY. It's almost seven, you know.
GILLETTE. (*Glancing at his watch.*) Is it? My God, you're right. I'd better hurry then, hadn't I? (*He exits up the stairs.*)

(*Pause. MAY glances coldly at LOUISE, avoiding her eyes. Then she finds her purse and begins to leave.*)

LOUISE. May.
MAY. I have to finish. (*She starts up the stairs.*)
LOUISE. May –?
MAY. (*Flatly.*) What do you want?
LOUISE. ...I want to apologize, for last night. I know you're angry...
MAY. Forget it.
LOUISE. I was trying to help. Didn't he tell you?
MAY. Yes. He told me.

LOUISE. Then it wasn't my fault, was it?

MAY. (*Cold.*) I guess not. (*Pause.*)

LOUISE. But you still don't like me.

MAY. ...No.

LOUISE. (*Turns away upset.*) If you had any idea how fond I was of Maude. How I miss her, what I've gone through.

MAY. You weren't suffering much last night, though, were you? In William's arms.

LOUISE. (*Pale.*) Did he tell you that?

MAY. No. I saw it. (*Pause.*)

LOUISE. ...You're jealous, aren't you?

MAY. Jealous? Don't be stupid.

LOUISE. May –

MAY. I'm not jealous –

LOUISE. May, listen. (*Pause.*) Last night...I was upset. I needed someone...But I don't love him. All right?

MAY. (*Shrugs.*) Fine.

LOUISE. (*Gently.*) May. Please. I'd much rather be friends with you. For Maude's sake. She would have liked that.

MAY. (*Relenting.*)...Do you think so?

LOUISE. I'm sure of it. I promise.

MAY. ...Were you really friends?

LOUISE. The best. (*She puts her hand to MAY's cheek and gazes at her. Pause. At this moment, LILLY and MARION enter down the stairs, both dressed for the party. LILLY is in a state. Hearing them, MAY breaks away from LOUISE.*)

LILLY. ...Well I just hate being late, but I always am. And it's so embarrassing...

MARION. It isn't late, dear. It's fashionable.

LILLY. May! Where are your shoes?

MAY. One minute. (*She hurries up the stairs.*)

LILLY. Well, hurry up!

MAY. (*Exiting.*) I'll be right down!

LILLY. Louise. Thank heaven somebody's ready. Now where's Leo? And Bobby...

LOUISE. They're inside.

LILLY. I should have started earlier...(*She heads to the dining room door, opens it and shouts.-*) LEO! TIME TO GO!

MARION. (*To LOUISE.*) That's quite a dress.

LOUISE. I'm glad you like it.

MARION. I hope it stays up.

LILLY. (*Returning.*) I always do this. Now let's just pray that we have enough gasoline.

MARION. Darling, it's not even a mile. We could almost walk.

(*LEO and BOBBY enter left.*)

BOBBY. All set!

LILLY. ...Now where's Willie?!

(*MAY hurries down the stairs.*)

LOUISE. He's upstairs.

MAY. I'm all ready...

LILLY. (*Calling up the stairs.*) Willie! Time
to go!

GILLETTE. (*Off.*) Coming!

BOBBY. (*Straightening his tie in the mirror.*)
Sarah, you know, has a real obsession about
younger men...

LILLY. (*Calling.*) We're running late, dear!

BOBBY. (*With a glance at MAY.*) And I must
say, I've always been attracted to older women...

GILLETTE. (*Enters at the balcony, wearing
his dressing gown.*) Well, you look a handsome
crew.

LILLY. (*Beat. LILLY is dumbstruck.*)
Willie! You're not even dressed!

GILLETTE. Yes, I know. I'm not going.

MAY. (*Crestfallen.*) You're not?

LILLY. Willie, what are you doing?

GILLETTE. Well, frankly, my arm's been
killing me, and I thought I'd just take it easy. (*He
descends into the room.*)

LILLY. (*At her wit's end.*) You can't do that!
They're expecting you!

GILLETTE. I'm sorry, dear.

LILLY. I told them you were coming!

GILLETTE. Now with all those people, they
won't even notice. Just give them my regrets, will
you.

LILLY. But we can't leave you. Not after last
night. It isn't safe. You know it isn't.

LOUISE. She's right.

GILLETTE. Oh, don't be silly. I couldn't be safer. After last night, I'm sure that our "mad gunman" wouldn't dream of trying anything.

MAY. You might enjoy the party.

GILLETTE. I'm sure I would, my dear. But not tonight.

LILLY. Leo. Do something.

LEO. Well...he's got a point. About the gunman, I mean. I'm sure he'll be safe.

LILLY. Leo!

LEO. But, on the other hand, you really ought to come.

MARION. A tower of strength.

LEO. Marion, if the man wants a quiet evening by himself, I don't see why he shouldn't have it.

MARION. Don't you?

LEO. No!

LILLY. Leo, you are no longer my favorite person.

GILLETTE. There. It's all settled. (*Pause. LILLY is defeated.*)

BOBBY. Well I'm ready to go. And I'm getting hungry.

LILLY. Oh, all right. (*To GILLETTE –)* But I'm very put out.

(*During the following GENERAL EXIT, MAY lingers behind.*)

LEO. We'll need two cars.

BOBBY. I'll take May, in the Torpedo.

LEO. Louise, you're coming with us. (*He offers his hand.*)

LOUISE. I'd be delighted. (*She takes his hand and they exit to the hall. MARION stalks out of the room behind them.*)

GILLETTE. (*To LILLY.*) You'll tell me all about it.

LILLY. I will not. And I'll be worried to death. I'll telephone you every hour. (*She exits.*)

BOBBY. May. Are you coming?

MAY. Hm? Yes.

BOBBY. Well come on. (*He exits.*)

(*MAY and GILLETTE are alone. She turns to him quickly.*)

MAY. Are you sure you won't come? I know you'd enjoy it.

GILLETTE. I'm afraid not. Now you have a good time.

MAY. But you shouldn't be alone. Really.

GILLETTE. I'll be fine. I promise. Just say hello to Sarah for me.

BOBBY. (*Off.*) May!? (*Pause.*)

MAY. Please?

GILLETTE. No. But thanks. (*MAY hesitates, then exits. GILLETTE follows her out the door. We hear them all in the hall, departing.*)

LEO. (*Off.*) Let's go.

BOBBY. (*Off.*) We'll follow you.

LILLY. (*Off.*) Willie, please be careful.

GILLETTE.   (*Off.*) I'll be fine. (*"Good
nights" are called from a distance.*)

GILLETTE. (*Off.*) Good night!

(*The front DOOR SLAMS. Silence. As
GILLETTE reenters, we hear the CARS in the
driveway, revving up. He closes the door
behind him, walks to the French doors and
looks out at the cars. Satisfied, he turns back
to the room. His movements now are
determined, business-like. He starts by
taking off his sling and tossing it away. He
flexes his arm, painfully, then walks to the
desk. He opens the top drawer and takes out
his gun. He snaps the barrel open and turns
the cylinder to confirm that it's loaded. He
snaps it closed.*)

GILLETTE. Maniac.

(*The LIGHTS fade.*)

End of Scene

Scene 2

That night, about 10 o'clock.
The stage is DARK. A MATCH is struck—
GILLETTE lighting his pipe. He sits alone

*in the darkness, on the floor, reclined
against the end of the sofa.*

*After several seconds, he hears a noise, off right.
He springs silently to his feet and moves
quickly, gun in hand, to the corner of the
room, down right.*

*He waits in the shadows. After a moment, the hall
door opens slowly, and MAY enters,
carrying her purse. She looks into the room,
sees no one, then walks quietly to the LAMP
next to the sofa and turns it on.*

GILLETTE. What the hell are you doing here?

MAY. (*Startled.*) Oh!...My God...

GILLETTE. (*Advancing, putting the gun back in his pocket.*) I said, what are you doing here?

MAY. (*Putting her purse on the table; avoiding his eyes.*) I—I just came back, that's all. (*Hesitates –*) I was worried about you.

GILLETTE. Oh, for God's sake –

MAY. I was worried! I couldn't stand it anymore.

GILLETTE. Did you come alone?

MAY. Yes. I walked.

GILLETTE. Good. Now I want you to go back.

MAY. To the party?

GILLETTE. At once.

MAY. But I just left.

GILLETTE. Yes, I realize that. You can take my car if you like —

MAY. No, I'm not going.

GILLETTE. May —

MAY. Why should I?

GILLETTE. First of all, because I want you out of danger. And second, because nobody's going to try a damn thing if they know you're here. Now with any luck, they won't have missed you.

MAY. You're waiting...for the killer.

GILLETTE. Of course.

MAY. Who? (*Beat.*)

GILLETTE. It's not your affair.

MAY. Not — ... How can you say that? She was my sister.

GILLETTE. Yes, I know —

MAY. I was almost shot!

GILLETTE. Which is why I want you out of here. Now.

MAY. Do the police know, too? Who it is?

GILLETTE. The police know nothing. Nineteen hours later and they've identified the gun. .38 caliber Remington. Single-action model.

(*MAY has started slightly at the name of the gun.*)

GILLETTE. Now I'm not going to ask you again. Do you understand?

MAY. Well that's ...fine. Because I'm not going.

GILLETTE. May –

MAY. I'm not. So just forget it. I'm staying with you.

GILLETTE. How dare you –!

MAY. (*Working herself up.*) I'm staying! And if you don't like it, it's just...just too bad. We're all leaving tomorrow, and you can...sit here, all alone...playing Sherlock Holmes. And you won't have to rely on anyone. Or trust anyone. You can do it all yourself! And get...blown to bits. And—bleed to death. But for tonight, I'm staying right here, so it's just too God damn bad!

(*He scrutinizes her. She's so upset that she's shaking.*)

GILLETTE. Do as you please.

MAY. (*Shaky.*) I will. Thank you.

GILLETTE. (*Continues to look at her.*) You're almost as stubborn as Maude was.

MAY. Well that's how it is.

GILLETTE. I'm very angry.

(*Pause. She's facing away from him. She tries to steady her voice, but she can't. She's too close to tears.*)

MAY. (*Quietly.*) I love you so much.

GILLETTE. May...

MAY. I do...

GILLETTE. (*Gently.*) May. Of course you don't love me. You're grateful to me –

MAY. You're wrong.

GILLETTE. You're twenty-six, my dear. We all think a lot of things at that age.

MAY. You're wrong.

GILLETTE. I'm fifty-one.

MAY. It doesn't matter.

GILLETTE. Trust me.

MAY. It doesn't matter!

GILLETTE. Of course it matters! You have your whole life ahead of you. You have everything to look forward to.

MAY. I don't want anything else.

GILLETTE. Of course you do –

MAY. I don't –

GILLETTE. Believe me –

MAY. You don't understand –!

GILLETTE. May! (*Brutally* –) Stop making a fool of yourself.

(*Pause. She turns away, mortified.*)

GILLETTE. All right?

MAY. (*Almost inaudible.*) Absolutely.

GILLETTE. (*Pause.*) I'm sorry.

(*Long pause. MAY remains turned away, rooted, staring at nothing. GILLETTE doesn't know what to say. Finally –*)

GILLETTE. Well...Are you hungry? (*No answer.*) May?
MAY. What?
GILLETTE. Are you hungry?
MAY. No.
GILLETTE. Well I'm starving. I'll go down and fix us something. Perhaps you'll change your mind. (*He walks to the hall door, turns.*) All right?
MAY. (*Still not looking at him.*) Fine.

(*He exits right, leaving the door ajar. MAY turns, angry and embarrassed. She walks to the door, hesitates, then slams it as hard as she can. Then she walks to the sofa and sits, trying to control herself.*
The room is silent. She sighs deeply...at which moment, we hear distinctly a SOUND on the terrace. A piece of furniture knocked to the ground. MAY starts. She listens. Nothing. She rises quickly and looks at the terrace. There's nothing there, at least that she can see. She looks at the door, right, wondering whether to call GILLETTE. No. She won't.
Slowly now, she walks to the French doors. When she reaches them, she hesitates. Then she turns the handle and pushes both doors open,

*gently, staying inside the room. She looks out
into the shadows.*

MAY. (*Her voice cracking.*) ...Who is it?
(*Silence. Pause. She takes a step forward. Then
another, crossing the threshold. Two more steps,
in total silence, and she's well onto the terrace,
her features in shadow. She looks to the right.*)
Who is it?...Is anybody AH! (*From the left, a
dark FIGURE leaps at her, grabbing her around
the mouth. She struggles in panic.*)

BOBBY. (*whispering excitedly.*) It's me!
Bobby! Now don't scream! Okay?!...Okay?!
AHH! (*She's bitten his hand.*) May!...

MAY. What are you doing!?

BOBBY. (*Overlapping.*) SHHH! Keep it
down!

MAY. (*Whispering.*) What are you doing
here!? (*During the following dialogue, which is
highly agitated, MAY reenters the room and
BOBBY follows her.*)

BOBBY. Where's Gillette?

MAY. He's in the kitchen.

BOBBY. Good. Now listen.

MAY. My God, I thought –

BOBBY. Just listen! You've got to get out of
here. Now.

MAY. Why?

BOBBY. We'll go to New York, I have the
car–

MAY. What are you talking about?

BOBBY. May, for God's sake. Just trust me! It hit me at the party, and then I couldn't find you —

MAY. What?

BOBBY. They weren't trying to kill Gillette, they were shooting at you.

MAY. Me?

BOBBY. You said it yourself. Last night, you were standing next to him —

MAY. Oh that's stupid —

BOBBY. I'm positive.

MAY. But who would want to kill me? It's —

BOBBY. That's what I couldn't figure. And then I remembered the letter. That explains it! (*He pulls out the letter that he took from her purse.*)

MAY. (*Pales.*) Where did you get that?

BOBBY. I took it.

MAY. Give it to me! (*She grabs the letter.*)

BOBBY. The point is that if it got around he'd be finished. He'd go to prison. So he has to kill you. (*Pause.*)

MAY. William?

BOBBY. That's what I'm telling you. (*Beat.*)

MAY. But that's impossible. He was here in the room. He got shot!

BOBBY. He must have hired someone. I don't know. He did it somehow. (*Desperate –.*) Maybe he meant to miss you, so when he killed you later, they'd never suspect him. I don't know. But you've got to leave.

GILLETTE. (*Off right.*) May! Could you get the door?

BOBBY. (*Freezes. Low whisper.*) Come on!
MAY. (*Low whisper.*) No!

(*BOBBY looks madly around, then runs to the French doors, pulls them closed, and darts behind the curtain, which hides him completely.*)

GILLETTE. May?!
MAY. Coming!

(*Uncertain what to do, she looks at the curtain, then at the door. She puts the letter on a table, hesitates, then goes to the door and opens it. GILLETTE enters carrying a large tray with both hands. The tray has plates, sandwiches, cutlery, etc. on it.*)

GILLETTE. (*Entering.*) The movable feast.
(*He goes to the coffee table, to put the tray on it, but it's covered with bric-a-brac: a lighter, vase, etc.*) May?
MAY. (*Distracted.*) Oh. Sorry. (*She goes to the table and makes room for the tray.*)
GILLETTE. (*The tray down, flexing his left arm.*) I made some iced tea, as well. It's next to the sink.

(*MAY is totally preoccupied. She stares at GILLETTE, considering.*)

GILLETTE. May?

MAY. Hm?

GILLETTE. Could you get it?

MAY. What?

GILLETTE. The iced tea. It's next to the sink.

MAY. Oh. All right. (*She doesn't move.*)

GILLETTE. It may need some more ice.

MAY. I'll get it. (*She hesitates.*) I'll be right back.

(*She exits right, leaving the door open. GILLETTE watches her go with a look of suspicion. Something's not right. He glances around the room and takes his gun from his pocket. He walks to the French doors and looks out. He is now about three feet from BOBBY. Silence. He sees nothing out of the ordinary. Convinced that something isn't right, he walks to the door left, peers into the dining room and exits.*

Immediately, BOBBY comes out from behind the curtain. With increasing panic, he looks around the room. What to do!? He needs a weapon. Then he sees it. He hurries to the bar and grabs one of the bottles, holding it by the neck. Satisfied, he hurries across the room and hides behind the door to the dining room.

A moment later, GILLETTE appears in the doorway, his gun back in his pocket. He eyes the living room again, then advances beyond the threshold. As hard as he can, BOBBY

smashes the bottle over GILLETTE's head.
The bottle shatters. GILLETTE staggers, then
falls to the floor, unconscious.
BOBBY stares at GILLETTE. Then he notices the
neck of the bottle still in his hand and tosses it
into the dining room. He kneels quickly and
grabs GILLETTE's legs. With enormous
effort, he manages to drag the body through the
door and out of sight.
Almost immediately, MAY enters right, holding
two glasses of iced tea. She advances into the
room—then realizes that the room is empty
and stops dead.)

MAY. ...William?...William? (*She puts the*
glasses down. With growing fear, she walks to
the curtain. Whisper.) Bobby? (*At that instant,*
BOBBY appears at the door left.)

BOBBY. May!

MAY. (*She whirls around with a gasp.*)
Where's William?

BOBBY. He...he went out. Now let's go!
Now's our chance! (*He hurries to the French*
doors. MAY, in the center of the room, doesn't
move.) Come on! We can be in New York in two
hours ...

MAY. The gun.

BOBBY. What?

MAY. The gun. Remington. Single-action.
How did you know?

BOBBY. What are you talking about?

MAY. That was the gun! Last night. How did you know? (*Beat.*)

BOBBY. I didn't. I mean, I heard the sergeant. On the phone. And I just ...said it.

MAY. (*Pause. She stares at him. She makes her decision. Calling.*) William!

BOBBY. May, stop it!

MAY. (*Growing panic.*) William!? (*She heads for the door to the dining room. BOBBY runs after her.*)

BOBBY. Now listen to me!

MAY. No!

BOBBY. (*He gets in front of her and grabs her by the shoulders –*) Listen!

MAY. No! (*She wrenches herself free and bolts into the dining room. He starts to follow her, but it's too late. Off.*) William!

(*MAY reappears on the threshold and stares at BOBBY. She's white as a sheet. She can hardly speak.*)

MAY. (*Almost inaudible.*) Why?

BOBBY. (*Quietly.*) May...

MAY. Tell me!

BOBBY. He was trying to kill you. (*He walks toward her.*) I couldn't ...let him.

MAY. Get away! (*She darts away, around the sofa.*)

BOBBY. May ...

MAY. Stay away from me! (*Panic stricken, she circles the sofa, her eyes searching the room for a weapon.*)

BOBBY. Just come here!... May...(*Suddenly she spots her purse, grabs it and fumbles with it, trying to pull her gun out. BOBBY runs to stop her, but he's too late. Gun in hand, she wheels around, just in time. He stops dead.*) May!

MAY. Get back! I'll kill you, I swear to God! (*Beat. They stare at each other.*)

BOBBY. (*Evenly, reasonably.*) May. Now give me the gun, and we'll talk about it. You know that I wouldn't hurt you. Why should I? Now just...hand it over...(*He advances toward her.*)

MAY. Get back! (*She fires, past his head.*)

BOBBY. (*Jumping backward.*) I'm back! All right! I'm back!

MAY. (*Breathing hard. Her voice is shaky.*) Now just...stay there. (*She thinks for a second, then realizes what to do. Keeping BOBBY in front of her, she backs across the room to the telephone.*)

MAY. Just ... don't move.

BOBBY. May, it's me. Bobby...

MAY. Stay there! (*She reaches the telephone, and has just picked up the receiver—when the DOORBELL rings. She starts. To herself.*) Thank God. (*Calling –*) Coming! (*She replaces the receiver and hurries to the hall door. Then she stops, realizing that she can't leave BOBBY. She hesitates. The DOORBELL rings again. Calling into the hall.*) Come around to the terrace. Can you hear me?! Come to the terrace. Hurry up!

BOBBY. For God's sake, if you'd only listen to me —

MAY. Shut up!

(*Pause. She watches the terrace, the seconds dragging. A few more seconds—then LOUISE appears.*)

MAY. Thank God.

LOUISE. (*Entering; seeing the gun, then BOBBY.*) May? What happened?!

MAY. It's him. He's the one. Who's been shooting —

BOBBY. Louise, listen to me. She's all wrong. I —

MAY. I know it!

LOUISE. Where's William?

MAY. He tried to kill him. Again.

LOUISE. Oh, my God.

BOBBY. It's not true! I just —

MAY. It is true! I saw him!

LOUISE. We should call the police.

MAY. I was just about to.

(*LOUISE goes to the phone and picks it up.*)

MAY. Where are the others?

LOUISE. They're still at the party—Hello? (*She clicks for the operator.*) Hello? ...(*Beat.*) It's dead.

MAY. Oh, no.

LOUISE. He must have cut the wire.

MAY. I think we should tie him up.

LOUISE. Good idea. There should be some rope in the kitchen. Or the basement.

MAY. I'll check. Here. (*She hands LOUISE the gun.*) All right?

LOUISE. I'll be fine.

MAY. (*Hurries out through the door to the hall. Exiting.*) I'll be right back!

LOUISE. (*Calling.*) Or get some clothesline!

BOBBY. Louise, now listen to me. She's got it all wrong. It was Gillette –

LOUISE. Stay back!

BOBBY. He was trying to kill her!

LOUISE. Just stay where you are! (*Pause.*) Now—now sit down. There. (*The chair. Beat. He sees that it's hopeless.*)

BOBBY. Fine. I'll sit down. (*He does.*) And when the others get back, maybe somebody will listen to me. (*A final attempt –*) You see, I found this letter—from Maude. She wrote it to May, the day she died...(*During the following, LOUISE walks toward BOBBY, then circles behind his chair.*)...Now I know this is hard to believe, but Gillette killed Maude. I know, it sounds incredible, but it's in the letter. Apparently there was someone else. She said he was jealous, that he hated her now and –

MAY. (*Off right, overlapping.*) I found some rope –(*She rushes in, carrying a cord.*) – but it isn't very - AHHHHHHH!

(*With a sudden, horribly violent blow, LOUISE strikes BOBBY on the back of the head with the butt of the gun. He slumps forward at the waist, then topples to the floor, onto his back.*)

MAY. Bobby! (*She rushes to him and kneels beside him.*) For God's sake, we could have tied him up! You didn't have to – ...(*She stops dead. Slowly, the truth dawns on her. She looks up at LOUISE. Pause. Almost inaudible.*) You.

LOUISE. May ...

MAY. It was you. (*Pause.*)

LOUISE. (*Quietly.*) I'm afraid so.

MAY. ...Why?

LOUISE. (*Quietly.*) Where's William?

MAY. I—I don't know.

LOUISE. (*Advancing.*) May. Where is he?

MAY. (*Retreating backwards.*) I...don't –

LOUISE. (*Maniacal.*) WHERE IS HE!? (*Pause.*)

GILLETTE. (*Quietly.*) Right here, Louise. (*GILLETTE is standing in the doorway, left, with his gun in his hand, pointed at LOUISE. At the sound of his voice, LOUISE swings around to face him, her eyes burning. She holds the gun in front of her. Quietly.*) Put it down.

LOUISE. Shoot me.

GILLETTE. I'm afraid I will, if you don't put the gun down. On the table.

(*LOUISE looks at the gun, then at GILLETTE. She hesitates.*)

MAY. (*To LOUISE.*) Please.

(*LOUISE turns and looks at MAY, who is almost beside her.*)

GILLETTE. (*Coming forward.*) May–!

(*In an instant, LOUISE grabs MAY by the hair –*)

MAY. No –!

GILLETTE. May! (*It's too late. LOUISE has the gun to MAY's temple. GILLETTE stops dead.*) LOUISE. Now drop it.

(*GILLETTE hesitates.*)

LOUISE. NOW!

GILLETTE. (*He has no choice. He tosses the gun onto the sofa.*) Now let her go.

LOUISE. Get back. (*GILLETTE doesn't move.*) Back! (*He backs up.*) I've waited a long time for this. A whole year...

GILLETTE. (*Quietly.*) It's me you want. Which is why you agreed to come here this weekend, agreed to the seance. I even made it convenient.

LOUISE. Very.

GILLETTE. Now, why don't you let her go?

LOUISE. It matters to you, doesn't it. She matters. (*Her attention turns to MAY and she pulls her head back, by the hair, causing MAY to gasp with pain.*)

GILLETTE. Louise!

LOUISE. (*During the following, LOUISE focuses increasingly on MAY, fascinated by her face. Increasingly, she identifies MAY with Maude.*) What an idea. I hadn't thought of this. You'd never forgive yourself. You'd have to live with it every day of your life. The way I did.

MAY. What are you talking about?

GILLETTE. Shall I tell her, Louise?

LOUISE. Shut up.

GILLETTE. (*Goading her; trying to distract her attention from MAY.*) She really ought to know...

LOUISE. I said shut up!

GILLETTE. May. Louise and your sister ...were lovers.

MAY. (*A murmur.*) Oh, my God....

GILLETTE. I didn't know. Maude fell in love with me, and Louise couldn't bear it. She begged Maude to stay with her. Then she threatened her, then shot her through the head.

MAY. No...

GILLETTE. Am I right, Louise?

LOUISE. (*To MAY.*) ... She loved me. She lived for me. Nothing else mattered...until he came, and took her away. We laughed at everyone. We used to sit on the bed and roar with laughter, until we cried. Because they didn't know. They never even dreamed...

GILLETTE. Then I came along. And took her.

LOUISE. (*To MAY.*) She was mine...I had to keep her –

GILLETTE. Louise!

LOUISE. She was mine!

GILLETTE. In the hospital, Louise. It was all true, wasn't it?

LOUISE. (*A whisper.*) Yes.

GILLETTE. She came to you that night. She stood there next to you, she whispered your name.

LOUISE. Yes...

GILLETTE. (*Advancing slowly, a step at a time.*) You could see her in front of you. You could hear her voice, the voice you loved. But you couldn't hold her –

LOUISE. (*A murmur.*) Stop it –

GILLETTE. You wanted to touch her again and feel her in your arms, her hair, her skin, her lips, you wanted to hold her, the way you used to –

LOUISE. Stop it –

GILLETTE. But she was dead. She was standing there but you couldn't *touch* her –

LOUISE. STOP IT!

(*She shoves MAY away from her, onto the floor, and FIRES at GILLETTE. MAY screams and GILLETTE halts abruptly. Pause. He stares at her without moving a muscle. Then he takes another step toward her. She FIRES again. He halts but doesn't fall. She FIRES two more shots, straight at him. He doesn't move.*)

GILLETTE. (*Quietly.*) It's all over.
LOUISE. (*She realizes now that he's unhurt, that the gun has blanks in it.*) I'll kill you...(*She backs away, dropping the gun to the floor.*) I'll kill you...(*In desperation, she looks behind her——and sees the dagger hanging on the wall. She darts to the wall, grabs it, turns, raises it above her head-*) I'LL KILL YOU! –

(*Suddenly a SHOT rings out. Then FOUR MORE in quick succession. LOUISE is thrown back against the wall by the force of the bullets entering her body. Still standing, she manages to see who shot her. She drops the knife, then collapses to the floor.*
MAY *is kneeling by the sofa with GILLETTE's gun in both hands, arms outstretched. She's in a state of shock. The gun falls from her hands, onto the floor.*)

GILLETTE looks at her for a moment, then strides quickly to LOUISE and bends down.)

GILLETTE. Louise...

(LOUISE slowly, raises her arms. She puts her hand behind GILLETTE's neck and raises her head, staring at him.)

LOUISE. ...She...loved me...

(She slumps to the floor.)

(GILLETTE looks up at MAY. MAY is dazed, shaking.)

GILLETTE. Are you all right?

(MAYtries to answer, but can't talk. She shakes her head yes and whispers "Fine." Pause.)

MAY. She...and Maude...
GILLETTE. I'm sorry.

(Then BOBBY groans.)

MAY. Bobby! *(She hurries to him and kneels down, as he groans again.)* Are you all right?...Bobby?

(*At this moment, the sound of a CAR is heard: TIRES SCREECHING to a halt, DOORS SLAMMING, etc.*)

BOBBY. (*Lifting his head, holding his neck.*) Oh, my God. (*The pain.*)

MAY. Here...sit up...

BOBBY. My God...(*MAY helps BOBBY onto a chair.*)

LILLY. (*Off.*) Willie!

LEO. (*Off.*) May!?

MARION. (*Off.*) Hurry up!

LEO. Lilly, be careful! Don't –!

BOBBY. (*Simultaneously.*) My head...

(*LILLY, LEO and MARION rush into the room from the hall. The following is jumbled, everyone talking at once.*)

LILLY. Willie! Willie, thank God!

GILLETTE. I'm fine, dear.

LEO. May!

MAY. I'm all right. It's Bobby –

MARION. We were scared to death. Lilly tried to call you and the line was out, so we jumped in the car –

LEO. God almighty. (*LEO has seen LOUISE. At his tone of voice, the others stop abruptly. They look at him and follow his gaze to LOUISE. Pause.*)

GILLETTE. She's dead, I'm afraid.

MARION. What happened?
MAY. She tried to kill him.
GILLETTE. She murdered Maude.

(*Pause.*)

LILLY. How horrible.
MARION. But why?
GILLETTE. Revenge. Love. It's a long story.
LEO. (*Finally.*) I suppose we should get the police. I can drive over.
GILLETTE. Yes. Of course. (*He exits to the hall.*)
BOBBY. (*In pain.*) I—I think I'd like to lie down.
LILLY. (*Focusing on BOBBY.*) Oh, dear.
MARION. What happened to you?
BOBBY. Good question...

(*MAY, MARION and LILLY minister to BOBBY: sit him down, wipe the blood from his face, etc.*)

MAY. She hit him.
LILLY. (*Wetting a napkin.*) Here. Get him some brandy.
MARION. I'll get it.
LEO. What the hell was he doing here?
MAY. He thought he was helping.
BOBBY. Ow!
LILLY. Sit still.

(*GILLETTE reenters, carrying a blanket.*)

MAY. (*To BOBBY.*) Can you walk?

BOBBY. I'm all right. (*He makes it, solo, to the center of the room; then he sees GILLETTE.*)

BOBBY. Gillette? (*Pause.*) I'm sorry. I mean, I wouldn't blame you...

GILLETTE. Go lie down. We'll get you a doctor.

(*BOBBY sways slightly; LILLY takes his arm.*)

LEO. (*To LILLY.*) Need some help?

LILLY. I've got him.

GILLETTE. Leo. (*GILLETTE and LEO cover LOUISE's body with the blanket, as LILLY helps BOBBY up the stairs.*)

BOBBY. It's my head...

LILLY. You'll be fine, dear. Hold on...(*BOBBY and LILLY exit.*)

(*The body is covered now and all eyes are drawn to it. No one really wants to say anything.*)

MARION. (*Finally.*) When I first met her, she was so beautiful, I thought—my God, if only I could be just like her.

LEO. Marion...

MARION. I did.

LEO. Well you shouldn't have. (*Pause. He holds her hand.*)

LEO. (*To GILLETTE.*) I'll fetch the police.

MARION. I'll go with you.

LEO. No need.

MARION. I'd like to, Leo. All right?

LEO. ...Right. (*Leo pauses for a moment, then realizes that MARION wants a moment alone with GILLETTE.*) I'll start her up. (*He exits through the hall door. Pause.*)

MARION. He told me why he wasn't in bed last night. We'd had an argument, about Louise, and he couldn't sleep. He sat up in the study...worried that I didn't trust him.

GILLETTE. Did you?

MARION. ...No. I guess not. (*Pause.*) Willie. I'm very sorry.

GILLETTE. Thank you, Marion.

MARION. You'll find someone else. You'll see.

GILLETTE. ...Of course I will.

(*MARION hesitates, then turns and exits. GILLETTE watches her go; the smile fades from his lips. He turns away. The room is silent. MAY is sitting, immobile, off by herself. Pause.*)

MAY. How did you know? About Louise.

GILLETTE. Maude's letter, primarily. "...If by any chance you ever learn the truth, I pray to God that you'll understand and forgive me."

MAY. (*Simultaneously.*) "—and forgive me."

GILLETTE. After that, everything fell into place. The seance, for instance. We'd arranged that I would speak with Maude, but Louise believed it, even then, that it really was Maude, and she couldn't help herself. (*Pause.*) And then the shooting—a year later, almost to the minute. As Leo said, it wasn't logical. In fact, it was barely sane. (*Pause.*)

MAY. (*Not moving.*) I...I suppose I should see how Bobby's doing.

GILLETTE. Of course.

MAY. Are you coming up?

GILLETTE. No. Not yet.

MAY. Oh. (*Pause.*) I'll see you later then.

GILLETTE. Yes.

(*She walks to the stairs and begins to go up.*)

GILLETTE. May – (*She turns.*) ...Tomorrow night, after the show...I thought we might...get some dinner. (*Pause. She stares at him.*)

GILLETTE. Nothing fancy...

MAY. (*Quietly.*) I'd like that very much.

GILLETTE. So would I ...(*A last look; she turns and exits up the stairs. He watches her go.*)... Watson.

(*The LIGHTS fade.*)

CURTAIN

COSTUME PLOT
(Period 1922)

GILLETTE

I. 1: Dark suit (as Macready), False whiskers and wig (as Macready), Leisure suitcoat (on chair).

I. 3: Trousers, Shirt, Slippers, Patterned silk dressing gown.

II. 2: Tweed suit, Traveling cape, Sling, Watch.

BOBBY

I. 1: Motoring coat, Motoring cap, Goggles, Leisure suit.

II. 1: Tuxedo.

MAY

I. 1: Coat, Dress, Purse.

II. 1: Dress, Purse, Party dress

LEO

I. 1: Overcoat, Leisure suit

II. 1: Tuxedo

MARION

I. 1: Overcoat, Leisure Dress, Purse.

II. 1: Robe, Party dress.

LILLY
<u>I. 1</u>: Hostess gown.
<u>I. 3</u>: Nightgown
<u>II. 1</u>: Robe, Evening gown with hooks up the back.

LOUISE
<u>I. 1</u>: Cape, Gown, Gloves, Shoes with mud stains, Purse.
<u>II. 1</u>: Robe, Evening gown.

PROPERTY PLOT

Furniture:

Wing-back chair
Ottoman
Electric gramophone (cabinet style)
Gramophone records
Side tables
Lamps
Telephone
Sofa
Chaise
Throw pillows
Clock that strikes the hour
Drop-leaf table rigged to make thumping noises
Seven chairs
Desk
Mirror
Portrait of Maude
Hidden bar
Curtains
Waste basket

Hand Props:

Persian slipper with shag tobacco
Deerstalker cap
Meerschaum pipe
Stradivarius

Scrapbooks
Dagger with jeweled handle
On bar:
    glasses
    liquor bottles
    towel
    spoon

Act I, Scene 1

Two five dollar bills (BOBBY)
Cigarette pack with two cigarettes (BOBBY)
Cigarette lighter (MAY)
Gun (MAY)
Gun (MACREADY/GILLETTE)
Suitcase with ruffle sticking out (LOUISE)
Ticket stub (LOUISE)

Act I, Scene 2

Cigar (BOBBY)
Cigar (LEO)
Hidden Projector

Act I, Scene 3

Glass of milk (LILLY)
Gun (MAY)
Letter (MAY)
Letter (GILLETTE)
Gun (GILLETTE)

Windows and wall lamp capable of shattering
Fake blood (GILLETTE)

Act II, Scene 1

Copy of *Variety* circa 1922 (BOBBY)
Tray with ice bucket and pitcher of tomato
juice (LILLY)
Glass capable of shattering (BOBBY)
Cigarette case (LOUISE)
Gun (GILLETTE)

Act II, Scene 2

Matches (GILLETTE)
Pipe (GILLETTE)
Purse (MAY)
Letter (BOBBY)
Tray with plates, sandwiches, cutlery and
napkins (GILLETTE)
Bottle capable of shattering (BOBBY)
Two glasses of iced tea (MAY)
Cord (MAY)
Blanket (GILLETTE)

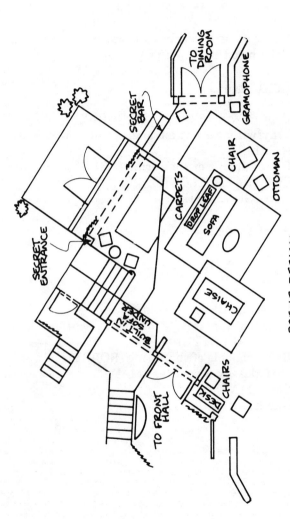

SCENE DESIGN

"POSTMORTEM"

LEND ME A TENOR
(Farce)
by KENNETH LUDWIG

4 male, 4 female

This is the biggest night in history of the Cleveland Grand Opera Company, for this night in September, 1934, world-famous tenor Tito Morelli (also known as "Il Stupendo") is to perform his greatest role ("Otello") at the gala season-opening benefit performance which Mr. Saunders, the General Manager, hopes will put Cleveland on the operatic map. Morelli is late in arriving--and when he finally sweeps in, it is too late to rehearse with the company. Through a wonderfully hilarious series of mishaps, Il Stupendo is given a double dose of tranquilizers which, mixed with all the booze he has consumed, causes him to pass out. His pulse is so low that Saunders and his assistant, Max, believe to their horror that he has died. What to do? What to do? Max is an aspiring singer, and Saunders persuades him to black up, get into Morelli's Otello costume, and try to fool the audience into thinking that's Il Stupendo up there. Max succeeds admirably, but the comic sparks really fly when Morelli comes to and gets into his other costume. Now we have *two* Otellos running around, in costume, and two women running around, in lingerie -- each thinking she is with Il Stupendo! A sensation on Broadway and in London's West End. "A jolly play."--NY Times. "Non-stop laughter"--Variety. "Uproarious! Hysterical!"--USA Today. "A rib-tickling comedy."--NY Post. (#667) **Posters.**

POSTMORTEM
(Thriller)
by KENNETH LUDWIG

4 male, 4 female . Int..

Famous actor-manager and playwright William Gillette, best known for over a generation as Sherlock Holmes in his hugely-successful adaptation of Conan Doyle (which is *still* a popular play in the Samuel French Catalogue), has invited the cast of his latest revival of the play up for a weekend to his home in Connecticut, a magnificent pseudo-medieval, Rhenish castle on a bluff overlooking the Connecticut River. Someone is trying to murder William Gillette, and he has reason to suspect that it is one of his guests for the weekend. Perhaps the murderer is the same villain who did away with Gillette's fiancee a year ago if you believe, as does Gillette, that her death was not--as the authorities concluded--a suicide. Gillette's guests include his current ingenue/leading lady and her boyfriend, his Moriarty and his wife, and Gillette's delightfully acerbic sister. For the evening's entertainment Gillette has arranged a seance, conducted by the mysterious Louise Perradine, an actress twenty years before but now a psychic medium. The intrepid and more than slightly eccentric William Gillette has taken on, in "real life", his greatest role: he plans to solve the case *a la* Sherlock Holmes! The seance is wonderfully eerie, revealing one guest's closely-guarded secret and sending another into hysterics, another into a swoon, as Gillette puts all the pieces of the mystery together before the string of attempts on his life leads to a rousingly melodramatic finale. " shots in the dark and darkly held secrets, deathbed letters, guns and knives and bottles bashed over the head, ghosts and hiders behind curtains and misbegotten suspicions. There are moments when you'll jump. Guaranteed."-- The Telegraph. (#18677)

New Thrillers from Samuel French, Inc.

ACCOMPLICE. (Little Theatre). Thriller. Rupert Holmes. 2m., 2f., plus one surprise guest star. Int. This truly unique new thriller by the author *The Mystery of Edwin Drood* broke all box office records at the Pasadena Playhouse, and went on to thrill audiences on Broadway. Sorry, but the only way we can describe the amazing plot for you is to "give it away." *Accomplice* starts out as a straightforward English thriller, set in a country house, in which a sex-starved wife plans, with the help of her lover, to murder her stuffy husband. All is, of course, not as it first seems. Oh, yes!—the "husband" is murdered onstage; but, later, he re-enters! Why? Because what we have actually been watching is a dress rehearsal. The play takes a new twist when we learn that this is an out-of-town tryout. The "husband" we have just seen "murdered" is actually the playwright and director of the play-within-the-play, and *he* has plotted to murder his *wife,* the actress playing the lead in his play, so that he can proceed unimpeded with his affair with her leading man. Got that so far? Well—you ain't seen *nothing* yet! A surprise character comes out of the audience (no—we won't tell you who it is), revealing that, in actuality, something entirely different is going on. A cast member is being set up—brilliantly and effectively, it turns out; and the cast has its final revenge against a fellow thespian whose cruelty resulted in the suicide of a friend. "The show is a delight. It is humorous, odd, scary, wildly dramatic, adult, adolescent—in short, impossible to dislike."—Pasadena Star-News. "Miss it at your peril."—L.A. Herald Examiner. "Wonderfully entertaining . . . a breathless ride through an ever-shifting series of planes."—Cleveland Plain Dealer. "A total delight."—Bergen News. "Part murder mystery, part sex farce and completely entertaining . . . suspenseful, charming and funny."—USA Today. Slightly restricted.   **(#3144)**

MAKING A KILLING. (Little Theatre.) Thriller. John Nassivera. 2m., 2f. Comb. Int. A Broadway playwright, his conniving producer and his actress wife hatch a plot to guarantee their new play will be a success; they fake the suicide of the playwright on opening night! They then high-tail it up to Vermont where the playwright hopes to disappear, as he hates the public spotlight anyway. However, after a few weeks the playwright decides he no longer wants to participate in the scheme. Maybe his wife and his producer (who are having an affair) will have to kill him for real! Also on the scene is the playwright's feisty agent, who uncovers the plot and then helps her client deal with his most difficult artistic challenge: foiling his producer and wife! "A magnificent mystery thriller ... wonderful entertainment."—Bennington Banner. "Absorbing theatre."—Schenectady Gazette.   **(#15200)**

Other Publications For Your Interest

PICTURE OF DORIAN GRAY, THE. (Little Theatre.) Drama. Adapted by John Osborne from the novel by Oscar Wilde. 11m., 4f., plus extras. I Int. w/apron for other scenes. English playwright John Osborne (Look Back in Anger, Inadmissible Evidence, The Entertainer) has given us a brilliant dramatisation of Wilde's classic novel about a young man who, magically, retains his youth and beauty while the decay of advancing years and moral corruption only appears on a portrait painted by one of his lovers. Following the advice of the evil Lord Harry, a cynic who, fashionably, mocks any and all institutions and moral precepts, Dorian comes to believe that the only purpose of life is simply for one to realize, and glorify, one's own nature. In so doing, he is inevitably sucked into the maelstrom of degradation and despair, human nature being what it is. "Osborne has done much more than a scissors-and-paste job on Wilde's famous story. He has thinned out the over-abundant epigrams, he has highlighted the topical concept of youth as a commodity for which one would sell one's soul and he has, in Turn of the Screw fashion, created a sense of evil through implication. Osborne conveys moral disintegration through the gradual breakdown of the hero's language into terse, broken phrases and through a creeping phantasmagoria."—London, The Guardian. "What is so interesting about John Osborne's adaptation of The Picture of Dorian Gray is that he had found in Oscar Wilde's macabre morality a velveted barouche for his own favorite themes. Osborne funks none of the greenery-valley vulgarity of the fabulous story, and conveys much of its fascination."—London, Daily Telegraph. State author when ordering.   (#18954)

FALL OF THE HOUSE OF USHER, THE. (Little Theatre.) Drama. Gip Hoppe. Music by Jay Hagenbuckle. 6m. 3f. Int. A comfortable suburban family man receives a desperate telephone call from an obscure and forgotten childhood acquaintance. Thus starts a journey into madness that will take Ed Allen to the House of Usher and the terrible secrets and temptations contained there. In this modern adaptation of the classic short story by Edgar Allen Poe, playwright Gip Hoppe takes Gothic horror into the 90s, questioning the definition of "sanity" in the same way Poe did in his day. Ed arrives to find Roderick in a state of panic and anxiety over the impending death of his sister, Madeline. As he tries to sort out the facts, he becomes tangled in a family web of incest and murder. Finding himself infatuated with the beautiful Madeline, his "outside life" fades from his memory as he descends to the depths of madness that inflict all the residents of The House of Usher. The Fall of the House of Usher is an exhilarating theatrical adventure leading to an apocalyptic ending that will have audiences thrilled. Actors and designers will be challenged in new ways in this unpredictable and wildly entertaining play. Cassette tape. Use of Mr. Hagenbuckle's music will greatly enhance the play, but it is not mandatory.   (#7991)

DEATH DEFYING ACTS
David Mamet • Elaine May • Woody Allen

"An elegant diversion."
N.Y. TIMES
"A wealth of laughter."
N.Y. NEWSDAY

This Off-Broadway hit features comedies by three masters of
the genre. David Mamet's brilliant twenty-minute play
INTERVIEW is a mystifying interrogation of a sleazy lawyer.
In HOTLINE, a wildly funny forty-minute piece by Elaine
May, a woman caller on a suicide hotline overwhelms a novice
counselor. A psychiatrist has discovered that her husband is
unfaithful in Woody Allen's hilarious hour-long second act,
CENTRAL PARK WEST. 2 m., 3 f. (#6201)

MOON OVER BUFFALO
Ken Ludwig

"Hilarious ... comic invention,
running gags {and] ... absurdity."
N.Y. POST

A theatre in Buffalo in 1953 is the setting for this hilarious
backstage farce by the author of LEND ME A TENOR. Carol
Burnett and Philip Bosco starred on Broadway as married
thespians to whom fate gives one more shot at stardom during
a madcap matinee performance of PRIVATE LIVES - or is it
CYRANO DE BERGERAC? 4 m., 4 f. (#17)

Samuel French, Inc.
SERVING THE THEATRICAL COMMUNITY SINCE 1830